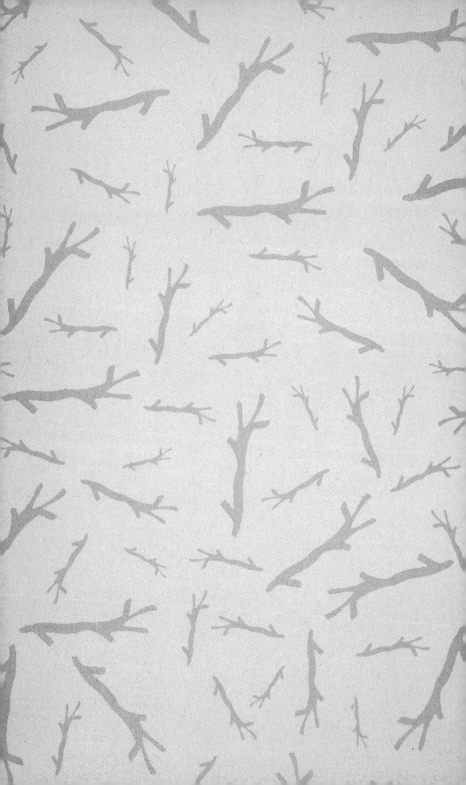

After the
River
the Sun

# After the River the Sun

## Dia Calhoun

Atheneum Books for Young Readers

New York   London   Toronto   Sydney   New Delhi

ATHENEUM BOOKS FOR YOUNG READERS
An imprint of Simon & Schuster Children's Publishing Division
1230 Avenue of the Americas, New York, New York 10020

ATHENEUM BOOKS FOR YOUNG READERS is a registered trademark of Simon & Schuster, Inc.
Atheneum logo is a trademark of Simon & Schuster, Inc.
For information about special discounts for bulk purchases, please contact Simon & Schuster Special Sales at 1-866-506-1949 or business@simonandschuster.com.
The Simon & Schuster Speakers Bureau can bring authors to your live event. For more information or to book an event, contact the Simon & Schuster Speakers Bureau at 1-866-248-3049 or visit our website at www.simonspeakers.com.
Book design by Sonia Chaghatzbanian
The text for this book is set in Goudy Oldstyle.
The illustrations for this book are rendered in collage.
Manufactured in the United States of America
0613 FFG
First Edition
2 4 6 8 10 9 7 5 3 1
Library of Congress Cataloging-in-Publication Data
Calhoun, Dia.
After the river the sun / Dia Calhoun. — 1st ed.
p. cm.
ISBN 978-1-4424-3985-6 (hardcover)
ISBN 978-1-4424-3986-3 (eBook)
[1. Novels in verse. 2. Guilt—Fiction. 3. Orphans—Fiction. 4. Uncles—Fiction. 5. Farm life—Washington (State)—Fiction. 6. Moving, Household—Fiction. 7. Washington (State)—Fiction.] I. Title.
PZ7.5.C35Aft 2013
[Fic]—dc23
2012023710

For Art Zink,
my father-in-law,
in honor of his life's work
creating a good, green place.
Gramercy.

## Acknowledgments

Trumpets are madly sounding for all the people who brought this book to life: Trumpets for Ariel Colletti, my editor, for inciting riots of creativity. Trumpets for Justina Chen and Lorie Ann Grover, brilliant authors and friends, for their willingness to fly to find me in dangerous places in the world and in the imagination. Trumpets for Sonia Chaghatzbanian, art director, for finding the perfect face for the book. Trumpets for Tyler Headley, for tossing me headfirst into the world of gaming. Trumpets for Sofia Headley, for keeping me in awe. Trumpets for Jim and Eva Calhoun, for raising me in a family where imagination was honored. Trumpets for Jill Anderson, for her insights on the manuscript. Trumpets for Bach, for writing the Chaconne in the Partita in D Minor. Finally, a fanfare of trumpets for Shawn R. Zink, my husband, for twenty-two years of being a lighthouse on a rock, whether in calm or storm.

# After the River the Sun

# PART 1:

# Hell's Canyon

# Chapter One

Eckhart rode a Greyhound bus
that charged down
the icy mountain road
like a knight's steed,
heedless of danger.
Lost in a game
on his Nintendo 3DS,
Eckhart didn't hear
the tire chains rattle,
didn't see
the snow pelting the window,
didn't think
about where he was going.
Instead he raced down a path
in an enchanted forest,
fighting demon-boars.

The game, The Green Knight,
concerned the adventures of Sir Gawain,
brave knight of the Round Table.
Faster and faster the demon-boars came—
springing from holes,
leaping from boulders—
and Eckhart slayed them all.
When fifty lay dead,
he found himself inside
the Chapel Perilous.

On the altar,
in a golden candlestick,
a candle burned
as brightly as the sun.
A grisly Black Hand
scuttled toward the light.
Eckhart tried to stop it,
but he needed the three knightly tools
of sword and spear and helm.
So far he had earned only the spear.

It wasn't enough.

The Black Hand smothered
the candle,

the light went out,
and Eckhart fell
and fell
and fell—
down
into death.

Eckhart paused the game
and stared out the bus window.
Death, he thought,
death was flinging him
out of a green city
to a new home
in the snow-shrouded desert.

No—
his blue eyes glared
back at him in the window—
not home,
never a home,
not without his mom
and the music leaping from her violin,
not without his dad
and his gut-splitting jokes.

The Greyhound bus

had rattled Eckhart
over not one
but two treacherous passes
in the Cascade Mountains,
heading for the high deserts
of Eastern Washington,
where he would live
with his uncle Albert.

Eckhart had never met his uncle Albert.

"Remember now,"
the social worker had said
when she'd plunked Eckhart on the bus
in Seattle that morning,
"your uncle is only taking
you on trial. So behave, be polite,
and do what he says.
Otherwise you'll be right back in foster care."

Eckhart knew all about trials,
because he had read stacks of books
about King Arthur
and the Knights of the Round Table.
Knights welcomed trials
and tests

and quests
to prove their courage
or honor,
or strength.
But what kind of tests,
Eckhart wondered,
would he have to pass
in order to stay
with Uncle Albert?

Eckhart would do anything
to escape foster care,
anything.
He had lived in foster homes
for the last four months
when he wasn't in the hospital.
How he hated it—
strange people,
strange beds,
and worst of all,
the strange smells of other people's houses.

Mrs. Shaw's house had smelled
of old clothes.
The Mathews' house had smelled
of Lysol.

Mrs. Johnson's house had smelled
of frying bacon
because she never opened the windows.
And everywhere Eckhart went
he had to protect his stuff—
especially his mom's violin—
from other kids.

Living with Uncle Albert
had to be better,
though Eckhart had doubts
about living in the high desert.
He would miss the rainy green of Seattle.
Why, he thought,
I'm just like Sir Gawain
before he became a knight.
Sir Gawain was wrenched
from the green land of his home—England—
and raised as an orphan
in a strange, foreign place.
At least, Eckhart thought
as his breath fogged the bus window,
there will be no rivers
in the desert.

But when the bus catapulted

from the mountains,
he saw that he was wrong.
The road followed a wide and brooding river—
the Columbia River, the bus driver announced.
Eckhart stared in dismay.
In some places
not even a guardrail
separated the road
from the riverbank.
He imagined the bus plunging
into the river,
imagined his arms and legs fighting
the ruthless current
as the black water swirled,
pulling him under,
drowning him.

His heart beating hard,
Eckhart turned away from the window.

A snore gargled and growled
from the man in the next row.
Only a few people rode the bus.
Eckhart reached for his phone
on the empty seat beside him
and searched through the photos

until he found his favorite—
his mom and dad and him
in their messy living room at home.

His mom was grinning,
her brown hair swept up
in the silver dragon clip
Eckhart had given her for Christmas.
She held her violin
and had just told them she was practicing
Pachelbel's Canon in D.
Cocking one eyebrow, his dad had said,
"I didn't know Taco Bell had canons."
Eckhart had doubled over
laughing on the couch,
his black hair hanging in his face.

Now, as the bus jounced,
Eckhart was filled
with a sudden wild longing to laugh—
until his body shook,
until his face squeezed tight,
until he gasped for breath.
But he hadn't laughed
in a long time.

Eckhart rubbed his thumb
over the screen on the phone.
His parents looked so real,
and yet so far away and frozen
behind the glass.
If only they hadn't gone
to Idaho.
If only they hadn't gone
rafting on the Snake River
through Hell's Canyon.
Then his parents would still be here—
and he would still be home,
*home*,
instead of on his way
to another stranger's house.

Why did they have to go and die?

Eckhart stared at a stain
scarring the bright blue cloth
on the seat ahead of him.
Then he picked up his 3DS
and started The Green Knight again.

Later, when the bus driver called,
"Town of Pateros,"

Eckhart looked up,
a little dazed.
He stuffed the 3DS inside his backpack
and picked up his mom's violin
in its black case.
The bus stopped beside a Quik Mart—
the town was too small
to have a real bus station.

The door hissed open.
Eckhart stepped out
into a February wind
so bitter and dagger-sharp
that he hunched his shoulders.
The bus driver pulled Eckhart's duffel bag
from the storage compartment
and dumped it on the snow.

Eckhart looked for Uncle Albert,
who was supposed to pick him up.
One other passenger got off the bus,
a girl wearing a white jacket
and silver boots that shone
so brightly,
Eckhart blinked.
He glanced at the sky—

grumpy with gray clouds hiding the sun—
then back at the girl.
What was making her boots shine?
She might be twelve, he guessed,
the same age he was.
When she smiled at him,
Eckhart froze.
A man with old-fashioned, gold-rimmed glasses
scooped the girl up in a hug,
then led her to a Ford pickup truck.

No one
came forward for Eckhart.

## Chapter Two

Standing beside the Quik Mart,
Eckhart watched the bus spit dirty snow
as it rumbled away.
Two cars sat in the parking lot—
a Subaru and a red Honda,
frosted like a cake
with three feet of snow.
It looked as though it had been left there
forever.

Where was Uncle Albert?

Eckhart eyed the river
beyond the parking lot.
Pateros sat where two rivers merged—
the bigger Columbia
and some smaller one

whose name Eckhart didn't know
and didn't want to know.
The Columbia brooded—
iron gray,
severe,
deep—
but the rabid wind licked
whitecaps on the surface.

He turned his back on it.

Maybe Uncle Albert was inside
the Quik Mart.
Eckhart slogged
through the gray slush.
He hated being out in the snow.
Even though his mom
had homeschooled him,
she had given him snow days off.
He'd spent the time gaming
or reading in his room—
not having snowball fights,
not building snowmen.

When Eckhart opened the glass door,
a bell jangled.

The Quik Mart smelled
of sour linoleum,
Comet,
and stale grease
from the fried chicken and cheese fries
in the display case.
At least it was warm.
Eckhart checked every aisle,
but saw no customers.

He held the violin case tighter.
Uncle Albert might have a flat tire
or be stuck in a snowbank.
All Eckhart knew about Albert Reed
were the stories his parents had told,
harsh stories—
about a man who was well-off
but who drank—
about a man who once had a family
but who now lived alone
on an orchard
in the middle of the desert hills.
How, Eckhart wondered,
pacing in front of the window
inside the Quik Mart,
could there be an orchard in the desert?

The store clerk,
a woman with brown dreadlocks
twisting like the roots of an old tree,
looked him up and down.
"We don't serve those here," she said.
Eckhart frowned. "What?"
"Your violin," the woman said.
"I imagine it drinks fancy Italian wine,
and we don't serve that here."
Eckhart blinked.
How had she known
his mom's violin was Italian?
The woman grinned. "Just a joke, hon."

He looked at her name tag—Alicia.
"Name your poison," she said.
"Cheese fries? Chicken? A Coke?"
Eckhart shook his head.
"I just got off the bus," he explained.
"My uncle is supposed to pick me up.
Can I wait in here? It's cold outside."
Alicia chomped a piece of gum.
"Sure, hon," she said.
"Just stay out of the way
of customers and ghosts."

Was she kidding? Eckhart wondered
as he wedged himself
between a newspaper stand
and a stack of Coke cartons
beside the front door.
After piling his duffel bag and the violin
at his feet,
Eckhart glanced out the window,
hoping to see Uncle Albert
drive into the parking lot.
But, except for the snow-frosted red Honda,
the lot was empty.

Or was it?

Where the Subaru had been parked,
something round and black
now lay on the slush.
Eckhart stared, puzzled.
Then he picked up the violin
and went out the door.
The freezing wind ripped back his hood
as he walked toward the thing
lying on the slush.

It was a round domed shell
about six inches across.
Then Eckhart knew—
it was a turtle.
The yellow squiggles on the black shell
sketched pictures in his mind—
a bud,
a flame,
a teardrop.

Eckhart had read
that turtles liked to bask in the sun.
This one might die from the cold,
if it weren't dead already.
A knight would rescue it.
Eckhart stretched out his hand,
then drew it back.
Would the turtle bite?
He bent closer.
The turtle's head,
like the rest of it,
was hidden inside its shell.
"How did you get here?" he asked softly.
"Maybe you just want to go home."
And he picked it up.

## Chapter Three

Cradling the cold turtle,
Eckhart carried it into the warmth
of the Quick Mart.
He hesitated,
then walked up to Alicia,
who was reading a book
propped on the counter—
*The Silmarillion* by J. R. R. Tolkien.
"Excuse me." Eckhart held up the turtle.
"I found this outside.
Do you think it's still alive?"

Alicia dropped the book
on the counter
and snatched the turtle
from Eckhart's hands.
"You found a box turtle
in the parking lot?" she cried. "Ooh,

he's so cold."

"But . . . is he alive?" Eckhart asked.

"Don't know. It depends how long
he was out in the cold.
Some stupid kid probably got tired of him
and just threw him away."
She clicked her tongue. "Left him
all by himself."

Eckhart stared down at the turtle.
Rage swept over him—
rage,
fear,
sadness—
until his breath clawed
in his throat.

Alicia said, "This fellow needs
to get warmed up—
slowly, though."
Eckhart's breathing eased,
and he nodded.
Alicia eyed the hot case
with the cheese fries and chicken.
"That would be perfect,
but I'd get fired if anyone found out.

I'll just tuck him in a towel
under the lamp in the backroom."
She glanced at Eckhart.
"You watch the store.
Holler if someone comes in."

Alicia disappeared through a door
marked EMPLOYEES ONLY.
Eckhart checked the time. Three o'clock.
Worry squeezed his chest—
could Uncle Albert have had an accident?
Eckhart couldn't even call him.
The cell service his parents had arranged
for him had just expired,
and there was nobody now
to renew the contract.
Besides, Eckhart remembered,
Uncle Albert didn't have a phone—
or a computer.
What kind of person
didn't have a phone or e-mail?

Alicia came back
through the employees' door,
her dreadlocks waving as she walked.

"Frodo has stirred," she announced.

"Frodo?" Eckhart asked.

"Sure. Perfect name for a turtle,
don't you think?"

Eckhart heard a motor rumble
and looked out the window.
An old pickup truck,
a brown, mud-spattered Dodge,
eased up to the curb.
Hunched over the wheel,
an old man slapped a yellow baseball cap
on his head.
An Irish setter with a gray muzzle
licked the passenger seat window.

Eckhart picked up his duffel bag
and the violin case.
He reached for the door,
then stopped and glanced at Alicia.
"Don't you worry, hon," she said.
"I'll take good care of Frodo."
"Thanks," Eckhart said.
She shook her head.
"The thanks goes to you,
for rescuing him."

Something bright flickered
inside Eckhart.
He looked at Alicia—
looked at her
and looked at her
and thought he might never look away.
Then the brightness faded.
She doesn't know, he thought.
She doesn't know what happened
in the river.
If she did . . .
she wouldn't . . .
Alicia smiled at him.
"Go on, then," she urged softly.
Eckhart took a deep breath
and opened the door.

## Chapter Four

Outside the Quik Mart,
Eckhart walked toward the man
standing by the truck.
As tall as a mountain,
the man wore faded jeans
and a brown wool shirt.
His arms dangled from his shoulders
like socks on a clothesline.
When Eckhart saw the blue eyes
glinting under the yellow baseball cap,
he caught his breath.
Those eyes were just like his mom's.
The same blue,
the same round shape,
the same glint—
though the glint had been more of a sparkle
on his mom.
This had to be his mom's brother.

"You that boy?" the man asked.
"Are you . . . my uncle Albert?"
Eckhart had not expected
such an old man,
such a run-down vehicle.
"I'm Eckhart Lyon," he added.
The man shook his head. "Eckhart.
What a name for a boy."

Eckhart flushed,
as he always did when teased about his name.
"It means," he said sharply,
"'the brave edge of a sword,' Uncle Albert."
"You'll call me Uncle Al," the man said.
"Get in the truck."
Eckhart slung his duffel bag in back.
When he opened the passenger door,
the dog didn't growl
but didn't move either.
Uncle Albert—Al—
got in on the driver's side.
"That's Cub," he said,
and pushed the passenger seat forward.
"Get in back, boy."

Eckhart hesitated.
Was Uncle Al talking to him or to the dog?
When the dog didn't move,
Eckhart shrugged off his backpack
and squeezed into the narrow backseat
with his mom's violin.
He had to sit sideways.
Uncle Al turned the key in the ignition—
the starter whined,
the engine sputtered,
and they started down the slippery street.

Eckhart couldn't see much
through the dirty windows.
Only desert to see anyway.
Only snow.
Only clouds.
Only nothing.
Here and there, tall trees
with bushy green needles
stood watch on the hills.

Eckhart closed his eyes
and pictured the old apple tree
that grew outside his bedroom window

at home.
When he was little,
he would climb out the window
into the branches and read for hours
about dragons
and knights
and perilous quests.
There, hidden by leaves,
sheltered by the tree,
he felt safe
in his own secret world.
After he started gaming,
he spent less time in the tree.
But gaming made him feel the same way—
safe in a world of his own.

How Eckhart wished
he were sitting in that apple tree right now,
the blue curtains fluttering
like banners from his bedroom window.
How he wished
he could hear his dad's voice calling him
to do his homework.
How he wished
he could hear his mom practicing her violin

for a concert with the Seattle Symphony.
How he wished
he could have his old life
back again,
be safe again—
the black, swirling hole inside of him gone.

Maybe Uncle Al's orchard
would have apples trees
like the one back home.
Eckhart pictured himself
climbing up and up
into the branches,
finding a secret place. . . .
That wouldn't be so bad.

Uncle Al didn't say a word
but clenched the steering wheel as though
it were the only thing in the world.
His right hand—
tanned and surprisingly smooth
for an old man's—
rested on top of the stick shift.
There was something about that hand
that Eckhart liked.

Eckhart's only other relative
was his dad's sister, Aunt Barbara,
who lived in New York.
Although she had flown to Seattle
when Eckhart's parents had died,
she'd left after the memorial service.
She was in college
and couldn't give Eckhart a home.
Uncle Al had not come to the service,
had not called,
had not even sent a card.
There had been only silence
until last week,
when he had sent the social worker a letter
saying he would take Eckhart on trial.

"We're here," Uncle Al said,
turning off the highway
onto a dirt road.
He drove up to a metal gate
that barred the way.
"Get out and open the gate," he said.
"After I drive through, shut it.
Don't want any deer getting in."

Eckhart shimmied out
from behind Cub
and stepped away from the truck,
his feet crunching on the snow.
Beside the gate
a sign with the words
"Sunrise Orchard"
in faded orange letters
creaked in the cold wind.
Below the words was a painting
of the sun rising over a hill.

Eckhart opened the gate,
and Uncle Al drove the truck through.
After Eckhart closed the gate,
his uncle yelled, "Just hop in back."
Eckhart hesitated.
Hop in back?
Ride with no seat belt?
"Hurry up!" Uncle Al called.
So Eckhart stepped onto the bumper
and swung over
into the back of the truck,
where he scooched into a corner
and held on tight.

Up a short hill they went,
Eckhart huddled against the cold.
Now he could see everything,
and the first thing he saw
was yet another river,
this one much smaller than the Columbia.
It looked cold,
surging over boulders,
the water swirling and eddying,
relentless in its rush
to some other place.

Eckhart didn't even have to listen
to hear its roaring,
because roaring was all he knew,
all he heard,
thought,
dreamed,
by day and by night.

Rivers—
hateful,
haunting rivers.
He could not escape them—
could not forget
what had happened

in that horrible gorge
at the bottom of Hell's Canyon.

When the truck crested
the top of a hill
and reached a flat stretch of land,
Eckhart looked eagerly
for the orchard.
Instead he saw a graveyard—
of trees.

## Chapter Five

Eckhart stared
at hundreds and hundreds
of fallen trees,
their dark branches
sticking up from the snow
like frozen spider legs.
The stumps, still in the ground,
showed that the trees
had once stood in rows,
had once been an orchard.

But it was all dead and desolate now.

Uncle Al drove the truck
up the winding, snow-plowed road
past row
after row
after row

of dead trees.
It looks like a wasteland, Eckhart thought,
from a fantasy book or game.

At last they reached a long
two-storied building
with weather-stained boards.
Four open bays stood on one end,
two bays with shut doors on the other.
Beside the building
was a white camping trailer
scarred with rust.
Uncle Al pulled the truck
into one of the open bays
and killed the motor.

Eckhart jumped out
of the back of the truck
and retrieved his backpack,
duffel bag, and the violin.
Then he looked at the building.
Was this his new home?
Did his uncle live
on the second floor—
or worse, in the rusty trailer?
But Eckhart's parents

had always said Uncle Al was well-off.
Eckhart had expected
one of those big cedar houses
with windows like pointed sails.

Uncle Al let Cub out of the truck,
plucked a bag of groceries
from behind the seat,
and said, "Come."
Again Eckhart didn't know
whether his uncle
was speaking to the dog or to him.
Uncle Al started walking with Cub
along a path crushed in the snow
that curved around trees
with blue-green needles.
Eckhart followed.

"That my sister Rose's violin?" Uncle Al asked.
Eckhart nodded.
Uncle Al glanced at him sideways.
"Worth a pretty penny, isn't it?"
Eckhart didn't answer,
but his hand tightened on the handle
of the violin case.
No one—

no
one—
was going to take
his mom's violin away from him.

It wouldn't be the first time
someone had tried.
A social worker had said
the violin was too valuable
to be entrusted to a boy.
She'd wanted Eckhart to sell it,
actually *sell it*,
and put the money in his trust fund.
Eckhart had refused,
arguing that his mom had paid insurance
on the violin for the next two years.
A judge had sided with Eckhart.

When he and Uncle Al
reached the other side
of the blue-green trees,
Eckhart saw a small house
covered with a metal roof
that gleamed as silver bright
as a knight's armor.
On the south side

the roof sloped steeply to the ground.
On the north side
the roof jutted out over a deck
that wrapped around the house.
The weathered wood walls
had windows of all different shapes—
round ones,
square ones,
angular ones,
and long skinny ones.
The whole place looked sturdy
but worn and neglected.

Then Eckhart saw something
that made him stop and stare.
Hanging from the roof over the deck
were stacks of curving pointed sticks—
antlers, he realized after a moment.
Held together with wire,
the stacks looked like antler trees.
Some of the horns were bleached white,
some were gray,
others brown,
all clacking in the wind.
"Did you . . . kill all those deer?" he asked.
"Some," Uncle Al said. "Most are sheds."

He stamped the snow off his boots
and went into the house.

Wondering what sheds were,
Eckhart stamped the snow
off his wet sneakers
and followed his uncle inside.
He entered a big room
with wooden beams across the ceiling.
Standing like a conquering king
in one corner
was a big black woodstove,
the coals glowing red
behind the glass door.
Copper sheeting protected
the walls behind it.
Above the stove,
hats, mufflers, and gloves
dangled from hooks on a beam.

The kitchen ran along
the left side of the room.
Shelves bristling with books
and the frayed yellow spines
of *National Geographic* magazines
covered the other wall.

In front of a window
a brown couch limped—
one corner propped up with bricks.
Eckhart looked around for the TV
but didn't see it.


"Bathroom's through there," Uncle Al said
as he put the groceries away.
"My room's across from it.
You'll sleep up there."
He nodded toward a spiral staircase.
"Get settled, make your bed,
and build up the fire.
I'll be in the shop."
And Uncle Al went out the door.


In the sudden silence
Eckhart stood,
just stood,
not looking at anything.
He felt like something stuck
to the bottom of someone's shoe,
wiped off in disgust,
tossed away.
He stood—
just stood.

## Chapter Six

All alone
in Uncle Al's house,
Eckhart noticed the sheepskin
hanging over the back of the couch.
His mom had owned one too.
He could see her now,
snuggled into it
as she read a book.
He walked to the couch
and rubbed the creamy wool—
it was warm,
it was soft,
it was something of home.

Taking a deep breath,
Eckhart stood straighter.
Then he looked at the woodstove.
Uncle Al had said to build up the fire,

but Eckhart had never
built a fire in his life.
They'd had no fireplace at home,
and he had never been a Boy Scout.
He decided to get settled first.

With his duffel bag in one hand,
and the violin case in the other,
Eckhart climbed up
the winding black metal stairs.
At the top
two shut doors faced each other
across a short hall.
He put down his stuff
and opened the door on the right.
Inside was a sagging bed
piled with boxes and stuffed plastic bags.
Eckhart opened the other door.

A big round window
let in a gulp of light
and a view of the snow-covered hill
to the south.
Beneath the window
a single bed with a striped mattress
stood on a faded blue rug.

A lamp sat on a broken chair
that served as a bedside table.
On the other wall
was a white bookcase
and a white chest of drawers.
A framed picture hung above it,
a child's crayon drawing.

Eckhart went over to look.
The picture showed a crooked house
with a blue heart-shaped door,
red flowers like lollipops,
and smoke poofing from the chimney.
Behind the house
a sun spiked with golden rays
was rising over a hill.
Eckhart liked the picture.
The name LILY
skipped across the bottom of the page
in crooked capital letters.
Lily, he knew,
was his cousin,
Uncle Al's only child,
who had died a few years ago.
Eckhart had never met her.

He decided this was the room for him.
Like a knight in a tower,
he could sleep
under the round window
and watch the stars.
Stars were one of the few things
about the outdoors he liked.

First Eckhart plugged in his 3DS
to recharge the battery.
Then he unpacked his duffel bag,
dumping his clothes
into the empty drawers
in the white chest.
The rest of his things—
mainly his schoolbooks—
had been shipped to Uncle Al.
Eckhart wondered if they had arrived yet.

Inside the closet
he found a box filled with sheets.
He opened a cedar chest,
breathed in its spicy scent,
and took out a red wool blanket.
After making the bed
he stepped back

with the pillow in his arms.

The red blanket looked warm and rich
beside the walls of golden wood.
Eckhart sank his nose into the white pillow.
It smelled as fresh
as the day the world was born,
as fresh
as though it had been dried
in wind and sunlight.
He laid it at the top of the bed.
Then Eckhart smiled.
He hadn't had a room all his own
since his parents died.
Maybe it will be all right here, he thought,
for a while anyway.
Until I find my real home.

His smile faded
when he looked at his mom's violin case,
still shut tight.
Sadness crept over him,
the furious,
unrelenting ache
for his parents.
He had to keep moving,

always keep moving,
to keep the sadness
from eating him up.
Eckhart slid the violin under his bed,
where it would be close,
where it would be safe,
but where he wouldn't have to look at it.

## Chapter Seven

Back down
the spiral staircase Eckhart went.
He hesitated,
then knelt before the woodstove.
How hard could it be
to build a fire?
After all, cavemen had done it.

He opened the glass door.
Red coals pulsed
in nests of ash.
Beside the woodstove,
in a crate that doubled as a table,
was a stack of logs.
Eckhart dropped one onto the coals,
then jerked his hand away
before it burned.
He waited,

but nothing happened—
the log didn't catch.

The front door creaked,
and Uncle Al came in with Cub.
"What are you doing?" he asked.
"Trying to get the fire going," Eckhart said.
Uncle Al shook his head.
"That fire's about dead.
You can't just throw on a log
and expect it to burn.
Add some kindling,
then fan the coals with the bellows."

Eckhart frowned.
What was kindling?
Then he remembered—
small sticks of wood.
He looked in the crate.
"But there isn't any kindling," he said.
"Then go chop some," Uncle Al said.
"The block and hatchet
are on the deck."

Chop some?
Eckhart's eyebrows shot up.

His parents would never
have let him use a hatchet.
They hadn't even owned one.
"I don't know how," he said at last.
Uncle Al stared at him.
"Time you learned, then.
Come on." And he went out the door.
Eckhart didn't want to learn,
but he didn't know what else to do,
so he followed his uncle.

Outside, the sun slinked
over the hills
in a glowering sky that seemed eager
to surrender the day.
Darkness was coming.
The cold wind crackled
against Eckhart's face.
Uncle Al stopped beside a stump
with a hatchet on top,
its blade biting into the wood.

When Uncle Al pulled out the hatchet,
Eckhart thought of King Arthur
pulling the sword from the stone.
Uncle Al pointed to the stump.

"That's the wood block."
He chose a small log
from the woodpile.
"Hold the log on one side," he said, "like so.
Then chop a sliver off the other side."
He swung the hatchet into the wood,
splitting it partway.
"Now you knock the whole thing
against the block.
That drives the hatchet
through the rest of the wood."
A stick of kindling
clattered onto the deck.
Uncle Al picked it up. "See? Try."

But Eckhart didn't like
the look of the sharp hatchet.
"I don't think my parents
would want me doing that," he said.
Uncle Al sighed. "Would they want you
to freeze to death?
Which would you choose—
death or fear?"

Eckhart's breath rushed in,
and he looked up sharply.

How . . . how could his uncle know?
Eckhart had not told anyone—
not the emergency rescue workers,
not the police,
not the social workers,
not the doctor,
not the psychologist,
not even his best friend, Ben,
what had happened that day
in Hell's Canyon.
Eckhart heard the water
roaring,
felt his hands gripping
the slippery log,
saw his mom's face in the water
as the current swept her toward him. . . .

"What ails you, boy?" Uncle Al asked.
Eckhart started,
then took a long shuddering breath.
No, he thought,
his eyes focusing
on his uncle's puzzled face.
No, he doesn't know.
Eckhart just stood,
staring at the hatchet.

Uncle Al sighed.
He swung the hatchet down
into the log again,
and again,
and the sound of splintering wood
rang high and hollow
in the darkening air.

Eckhart looked out.
The rows of dead trees,
ghostly now in the dusk,
made him feel as though rocks
were piled on his chest.
But not far from the house,
across a sweeping snowy lawn,
four trees still stood
against the bottom of the southern hill.
Their branches were bare,
yet they seemed to defy
the cold,
the snow,
and the approaching winter night.

They're still alive,
Eckhart thought,
somewhere deep down.

He imagined climbing
into the branches,
climbing up and up
as the tree soared
like the magical Christmas tree in *The Nutcracker*.
He would keep climbing
until he found
a bright new home.
He would keep climbing,
and neither cold nor darkness
would defeat him.

Then Eckhart felt his heart beating,
beating hard,
as his uncle chopped the kindling
that would bring the fire
alive again.

## Chapter Eight

Back inside the house
Uncle Al showed Eckhart
how to use the kindling
and bellows to build up the fire.
When flames curled over the wood,
Uncle Al said, "Supper time.
Can you at least set a table?"
Eckhart nodded.
Of course he could set a table.
That had been his job at home
since he was seven years old.

He opened the cupboards—
painted bright blue—
until he found what he needed.
Chipped, mismatched plates.
Knives, forks, and spoons.
He set them on the table.

Since there were no napkins,
he folded paper towels
neatly in half.

When the table was ready,
Eckhart stood back.
"Uncle Al," he said,
"there's only one chair."
Uncle Al opened a bottle of beer
and looked at the table.
"So there is. There's a crate
on the deck, by the antlers.
You can use that for now.
Fetch it."

Eckhart found the crate,
carried it inside,
and sat down slowly,
looking at his plate in dismay.
Kidney beans baked
with sliced hot dogs
covered half the plate.
A pile of corn
and a slab of bread
lay beside the beans.
Swallowing hard,

Eckhart gripped his fork,
the stink of beans rising into his nose.
He ate
every bite of the corn,
every bite of the hot dogs,
every bite of the bread.

He didn't touch the beans.

Uncle Al said,
"The social worker says you got pneumonia
after the accident. That true?"
Eckhart nodded.
Uncle Al took a long drink
from his second beer.
"She said the doctor wants you out
of school till spring—
or even fall.
Wants you to rest
and get your health back."

Eckhart felt relieved.
It would have been hard
starting at a new school
in the middle of the year,
hard to make friends.

"But," Uncle Al added, "you must
keep up your studies in your workbooks.
I'll be checking.
You'll have chores, too."
He slathered butter as thick as icing
on a piece of bread.
"Still," he said, "you'll have time for yourself.
There's plenty to explore around here."

Eckhart pictured himself
wandering alone
through the dead orchard,
his footprints leaving empty places
in the snow.
"What kind of trees were those?" he asked.
"All those trees lying dead
on the ground?"
A shadow crossed his uncle's face.
"Pears, a variety called Bartletts."
"What happened?" Eckhart asked.
"Why are they all dead?"
His uncle gripped the beer bottle.
"'Cause I ripped them out."

Speechless,
Eckhart stared at his plate,

scared to look at his uncle.
He wanted to ask why
his uncle had ripped out
the pear trees,
but he didn't dare.

Uncle Al asked, "Something wrong
with your beans?"
"No," Eckhart said.
"I just can't eat them."
Uncle Al raised his eyebrows.
"What do you mean?"
Eckhart poked the rusty-colored beans
with his fork. "I just can't . . .
eat beans."
A silence fell,
stretching on and on
until it seemed to snarl.

Uncle Al sighed. "Best to begin
as we mean to go on.
Cleaning your plate is a rule here."
Eckhart stared at the black window—
no curtains shut out the night.
"I can't," he said.
"I'll eat anything else.

But not beans."
Uncle Al's chair screeched
against the linoleum
as he pushed it away from the table.
"Then get up to bed."
"Bed?" Eckhart protested.
"But it's not even seven o'clock."
Uncle Al looked at him.
"Clean your plate or go to bed.
It's your choice."

Eckhart jumped up.
He wanted to
throw
the stinking plate—
smash
the terrible beans—
kick
the stupid crate—
but he stomped toward the spiral staircase.
When he was halfway up,
his uncle called, "I'll wake you at five."
Eckhart stopped,
his foot frozen above the next stair.
Five? Five o'clock in the morning?
He took a deep breath,

then marched on up the stairs.

When he opened the door to his room,
a blast of cold slapped him.
If he left the door open,
the room would warm up,
but he shut it behind him,
shut it hard,
and leaned back against it.
I won't stay here, he thought.
"By my troth," he said—
an expression knights used
to pledge their sworn word—
"I won't.
This isn't home.
It will never be home."

As the cold crept over him,
Eckhart thought of Frodo.
He wondered
if Frodo had warmed up under the lamp,
if Alicia had fed him,
smiled at him.
He yanked open a drawer in the white chest,
pulled out his pajamas,
and put them on fast.

Lily's picture gleamed on the wall—
the crooked house,
the lollipop flowers.
When he touched the rising sun,
the glass felt cold.

His 3DS had recharged.
Eckhart turned on his iPod,
stuffed in his earbuds,
and selected the *Devil's Trill* Sonata
by Tartini.
As the menacing notes played,
he pulled back the red wool blanket
and the white sheet
and burrowed into bed.
Then he started The Green Knight.

Racing
down the twisting corridors
of the Chapel Perilous—
searching
for the sword
that would keep the Black Hand
from snuffing out the candle—
Eckhart forgot
about the trial,

forgot
about his parents' death,
forgot
every horrible thing
that had happened to him
in the last four months.
As the fiery cadenza exploded
at the end of the sonata,
he at last found his sword
stuck fast in a dead tree.

Two hours later
Eckhart turned off the 3DS.
He hadn't found a way
to pull out the sword.
Sleepy at last,
he lay down
and watched the winter stars
glimmer outside the round window.
Strange sounds spilled from the night—
the hooting
of an owl,
the creaking
of the wooden house,
the skittering

of some creature
on the deck below.
Then Eckhart heard
the river roaring in the distance.

It was merely a whisper
of the thunderous roaring
he had heard on the Snake River
that day in Hell's Canyon.
But as Eckhart listened,
the roaring seemed to grow louder,
as though the river were screaming
at him,
trying to leap from its banks
and come for him
as it did every night
in his dreams.

Howling ripped the air,
loud and close.
Eckhart sat straight up.
Yips and barks
shrilled and snapped.
Was a pack of dogs running loose?
The mournful howling

went on
and on,
and as it did,
Eckhart felt an answering howl
rise inside his own chest.

He lay down again.
A line from his favorite book,
*The Boy's King Arthur*,
flashed in his mind:
*And there he lay all that night*
*without comfort of anybody.*
Sir Lancelot had been alone too,
a captive in the Castle Chariot.
Eckhart pulled the red wool blanket
up to his chin,
desolate
at the thought of life here
on this dead orchard,
with this strange man.

Would he ever find a real home?

Suddenly the stars beating down
were too bright,
the river too loud.

Eckhart pulled the pillow
over his head,
but he couldn't hide
from the brightness
and the roaring.

## Chapter Nine

Hours later,
Eckhart was screaming
as the Black Hand
tried to drag him underwater.
"Wake up!" a voice exclaimed.
"You're dreaming, boy."
Gasping, Eckhart opened his eyes.
It was Uncle Al's hand on his shoulder,
shaking him awake—
not the Black Hand.
Eckhart took a deep breath.

Uncle Al flicked on the light.
"Heard you all the way downstairs."
Eckhart sat up,
and Uncle Al looked at him sharply.
"You have a lot of nightmares?"
Eckhart nodded, rubbing his eyes.

Uncle Al seemed about to say something more,
then stopped.
"What time is it?" Eckhart asked.
"Nearly five. You might as well get up."
And Uncle Al left the room.

Eckhart glanced out the round window.
The sky was still dark,
and the stars still shone.
Shaking off the nightmare,
he pulled on his clothes
in the freezing room.
Then, yawning,
he walked down the spiral staircase
into the warm air.
Flames snapped
behind the glass window
in the woodstove.
Cub basked in the heat
on an old rug.
Holding a coffee cup,
Uncle Al flipped pancakes
that smelled of cinnamon
on a sizzling griddle.
Eckhart was glad that breakfast wasn't beans.

But it was.
For there, waiting on the table,
sat the plate of beans
he had refused to eat the night before.
They looked terrible—
cold, the fat congealed like glue.
Slowly Eckhart eased onto the crate
and stared at the beans.

Uncle Al sat down
with a plate of pancakes.
He poured maple syrup
on one of them,
spooned on cottage cheese,
and then slapped another pancake on top.
He kept layering—
syrup,
cottage cheese,
pancakes,
until he had a stack four high.

Eckhart scowled at the beans
on his own plate.
All right.
If this was what he had to do
to stay out of foster care—

just eat some stupid beans—
all right then.
Sir Gawain would do it laughing.
Eckhart picked up his fork,
scooped up some beans,
and stuffed them into his mouth.

As he chewed,
the stink of the beans
clouded around his head.
The lumpy mush in his mouth
tasted like death.
Eckhart swallowed fast and hard,
then stared miserably down
at all the beans left on his plate.
How many were there?
Fifty? A hundred? Two hundred?
His stomach heaved.
Eckhart sprang off the crate,
ran into the bathroom,
and threw up in the toilet.

Uncle Al came
and stood in the bathroom doorway.
"What is the matter with you?" he demanded.
"I told you!" Eckhart shouted.

"I told you—
I
can't
eat
beans!
Not anymore."

Uncle Al frowned. "Why?"

Eckhart blinked at the toilet seat.
"That—that . . . day," he stammered.
"We had lunch—
before the accident.
Baked beans.
I . . . It . . . They . . ." He stopped,
fighting tears,
but one ran down his cheek.

Uncle Al asked, "Just what happened
that day anyway?"
Eckhart heard the roar
of the river,
saw the beans he had thrown up
in the river,
saw them torn away
by the river.

His eyes focused
on the beans floating in the toilet,
and he threw up again.

To Eckhart's surprise
Uncle Al brought him a glass of water.
"Drink that," he said gruffly.
"Then brush your teeth
and come back to the table."

After finishing in the bathroom
Eckhart walked back to the kitchen.
He wouldn't eat one more bean.
He didn't care if his uncle starved him—
he would never eat beans again.
But the beans were gone.
In their place was a plate
heaped with pancakes.

Surprised again,
Eckhart glanced at his uncle,
but his uncle snapped the lid
on the cottage cheese tub
and didn't look back.
So Eckhart reached for the syrup.
He poured a golden stream

over his pancakes.
When he took a bite,
sweetness soaked his tongue,
and his eyes lit up—
it was real maple syrup.
Eckhart had only tasted real maple syrup
once before.
His parents had always
bought Mrs. Butterworth's.

"These pancakes are good," Eckhart said.
Uncle Al sipped his coffee.
"Don't sound so surprised."
Eckhart sat back on the crate.
"Why were those dogs
howling outside last night?"
"Not dogs," Uncle Al said. "Coyotes."
Eckhart's fork froze in the air.
"Coyotes? But they were so close.
Aren't they dangerous?"
Uncle Al shook his head.
"Coyotes don't eat people.
Only mice, rabbits, and fruit.
Deer when they can get them."
Eckhart eyed his uncle doubtfully,
then started eating again.

As he ate his pancakes,
as he tasted
the sweet maple syrup—
as he felt
the warmth of the snapping woodstove—
as he thought
of his very own room with its red wool blanket
and its pillow that smelled of sun and wind—
Eckhart made a decision.
He would stay at Sunrise Orchard,
for now anyway,
because it was better than foster care.

Eckhart glanced at his uncle,
wanting to ask about the trial.
What would the tests be?
How long would the trial last?
He needed to know
what he had to do
so he wouldn't be sent away.

But Eckhart was afraid to ask.

## Chapter Ten

After the breakfast dishes
were washed and put away
in the blue cupboards,
Eckhart looked out the front window
and wondered if dawn would ever come.
He couldn't remember the last time
he'd been up this early.
No, wait. He did remember—
the morning he and his parents
had risen at four a.m.
to catch the plane from Seattle,
the plane that had taken them
to Hell's Canyon.

Eckhart knew why his dad
had chosen the rafting trip for their vacation—
to tear Eckhart away
from his gaming and reading.

It hadn't been his mom's idea.
She'd hated the outdoors
as much as Eckhart did.
Not once had they ever
gone camping or fishing.
If only they had gone to New York City
and visited the museums.
If only they had gone to a fantasy
and gaming conference.
If only they had done anything else,
anything at all.
If only . . .

Outside, the darkness was lifting.
To the south
the four trees still standing
huddled against the hill.
To the east
the dead Bartlett trees
looked like ghostly phantoms
that might reach out
and drag him under.

Eckhart sighed.

He turned away

from the coming dawn
and saw Uncle Al leaning
against the kitchen counter,
watching him.
"It's your first day," Uncle Al said.
"Go out and explore
before you start your schoolwork."
Eckhart shrugged. "I'd rather play
computer games. Or read."
Uncle Al shook his head.
"You need air and exercise."
Eckhart shoved his hands in his pockets.
"But I hate the outdoors."

To Eckhart's surprise
Uncle Al threw back his head and laughed.
His laughter had a sharp edge—
like the hatchet, Eckhart thought.
"Ridiculous," Uncle Al said
when he'd finished laughing.
"A boy who hates the outdoors?
What was Rose thinking,
raising you that way?
She always was a strange one."

"Stop it!" Eckhart exclaimed.

"Don't say bad things about my mom!"
As soon as the words were out,
he wanted to stuff them back in his mouth.
If Uncle Al became angry,
he might end the trial
before it even began
and send Eckhart back to foster care forever.
But again Uncle Al surprised him.
"Good boy," he said, nodding.
"A boy should always stand up for his mother.
Now fetch your jacket.
You've got an appointment
with a pair of snowshoes."

Ten minutes later,
with a pair of snowshoes
strapped to his boots,
Eckhart stepped forward—
and fell
down into the snow.
Cold gnawed his cheek.
He decided he might just stay
on the ground forever.
Uncle Al said, "The tip of your snowshoe
dug into the snow. Get up."
Scowling, Eckhart climbed to his feet

and slapped snow from his jeans.
He didn't want to be doing this.

"Keep the toes up," Uncle Al advised,
"and slide your feet. Try again."
Eckhart slid his right leg forward
and stamped it down.
It worked.
He picked up his left leg,
took another halting step,
and then another
and another.

The sun had risen.
The western sky glimmered,
pink and gold—
as feathery
as the wings of an angel.
Slowly,
laboriously,
Eckhart tramped across the snow
to the four trees
at the bottom of the south hill.
Uncle Al followed.

"Are these pear trees too?" Eckhart asked.

"They're peaches," Uncle Al said.

"Do you sell them?"

"Sell them?" Uncle Al looked outraged.

"Those are Lily's peaches.

I wouldn't sell a one."

His shoulders hunched,

Uncle Al walked away

toward the shop building.

Eckhart looked longingly up

at the round window of his room,

but his uncle had told him

to stay outside for at least an hour.

An hour seemed like forever.

Eckhart wondered where to go next.

A path to the south

ran between a hill

and the dead orchard.

The snow wasn't so deep there,

so he set off

to see where the path led.

At first it ran downhill,

making snowshoeing easy.

But then the path sloped upward,

and Eckhart began to pant.

He hated exercising—
the panting,
the sweating,
the pounding, breathless heart.
This had led to many arguments
with his dad,
who'd always wanted
Eckhart to go jogging with him.

The path ended.
Only deep snow lay before him.
He checked his watch—
still a half hour left.
So out into the deep snow he went,
tramping beside a wire fence
that stood nine feet high.
On the other side of the fence,
a real orchard grew—
its bare trees in orderly rows.
Thickets of shoots sprouted
from the branches.
Eckhart spotted a man in the distance.
He was perched on a ladder,
snipping off the shoots
with a cutter on a long pole.
Pruning, Eckhart remembered.

Pruning was the word
for trimming trees.

He passed a little gate in the fence,
one so low,
it might have been used by the dwarves
in *The Lord of the Rings*.
Then the land crested a rise,
and Eckhart saw the river
in all its coldness,
brooding like a monster
trapped between icy banks.

As Eckhart stood watching it,
he thought of all he didn't know
about what his life
would be like now.
But he knew two things for certain.
First, his mom had died
knowing her son was a coward—
and second,
he would never
be able to forget that,
not ever.

Eckhart turned away

from the river
and slogged
on the snowshoes
back toward the house.
The trials Uncle Al set for him
had better be hard,
had better be impossibly hard,
because Eckhart wasn't sure—
wasn't one bit sure—
that he deserved any kind of home at all.

## Chapter Eleven

Later that afternoon
Eckhart sprawled on the rug
in front of the woodstove,
working in his math book.
He crossed out yet another wrong answer
and then hurled his pencil
across the room.
It slammed against the wall.

Usually he liked math,
but all he could think about now
were all the chores
Uncle Al had shown him after lunch.
Eckhart had to
shovel snow off the path to the house.
Eckhart had to
bury the table scraps in the dead orchard.
Eckhart had to

check that the front gate was closed at dusk.
Eckhart had to
trundle logs from the shop building
and stack them in the woodpile on the deck.
All of it was outside work,
all boring,
nothing noble and glorious
that a knight would do
to prove himself on a trial.

Eckhart retrieved the pencil
and erased the mark on the wall.
Luckily, Uncle Al had stepped outside.
Eckhart cast a longing look
at the spiral staircase,
thinking of the 3DS and The Green Knight
waiting in his room.
There had to be a way to pull the sword
from that dead tree.
But Uncle Al had told him to work downstairs—
"Where I can keep an eye on you."
Sighing, Eckhart flopped back on the rug.
Cub, sprawled beside him,
began to snore
as Eckhart attacked the math problem again.

He had solved three problems,
when men's voices rang outside.
Footsteps bumped across the deck,
stomping snow off boots.
The door creaked opened,
shooting cold inside,
and two men came in with Uncle Al.
"Coffee's on," Uncle Al said.
"Take off your coats and sit."
He nodded toward the brown couch
with the sheepskin.

The men saw Eckhart on the floor
and stopped.
One of them,
tall and thin,
was the man who had met
the girl in the shining boots
at the bus stop in Pateros.
He smiled at Eckhart. "Why, who's this, Al?"
"What?" Uncle Al glanced at Eckhart
and blinked as though he, too,
were surprised to see him there.
"Oh. My nephew."

The other man had a brown face
under a grizzled beard.
He unwound a green muffler
layer by layer—
like a peeling mummy, Eckhart thought.
The bearded man asked, "Does your nephew have a
name, Al?"
Uncle Al sighed. "Eckhart Lyon.
Unfortunate but true."
Eckhart felt his cheeks grow hot.
To hide his embarrassment
he petted Cub,
who rolled over onto his back
to have his belly scratched.

The tall man pushed up
his old-fashioned, gold-rimmed glasses.
"Hello, Eckhart," he said.
"Our names are similar.
I'm Mr. DeHart. I live on the orchard
to the north, Acadia Orchard.
And this is Mr. Salinas.
He owns the orchard just south of here.
My daughter, Eva, is about your age."
"Hello," Eckhart said,

wondering if Eva was the girl
in the shining silver boots.

After Uncle Al handed the men
cups of steaming coffee,
he pulled up the chair from the table
and sat across from them.
The men sipped their coffee
and discussed the weather.
Then a silence fell.

"Well?" Uncle Al asked.
"You probably know," Mr. DeHart said,
"why we're here."
Uncle Al nodded. "I can guess."
"It's been three years," Mr. Salinas said,
"since you cut down the pears.
The shoots and brush have sprouted up
faster than dazes.
You're not spraying it, Al,
so the place is a breeding ground
for fire blight, pear psylla, and mice."
"And," Mr. DeHart added,
"it all scoots right over the deer fence
and reeks havoc in our orchards."

Mr. Salinas jabbed a finger at Uncle Al.
"I lost a good fifteen percent
of last year's crop because of your mess.
And this year will be even worse
because of the mild winter."
Mr. Salinas's cheeks puffed out.
"I'm not putting up with it anymore.
I'll get the law on you if—"
Mr. DeHart gripped Mr. Salinas's arm
and said, "Let's just stay calm."
Mr. Salinas shook his head,
then quieted and sipped his coffee.
"Look, Al," Mr. DeHart said.
"You've been a good neighbor for years.
We're just asking you to clean up your mess.
We don't want to complain
to the Pest Control Board,
but we will if we have to."

Uncle Al looked up sharply
but didn't say anything.
"Three years, Al," Mr. DeHart added softly.
"Isn't that long enough to blame yourself?"
Startled, Eckhart glanced at his uncle.
What was he blaming himself for?
Uncle Al took another sip of coffee,

but his cup was empty.
He stared into it
as Mr. Salinas cleared his throat.
"We, uh, we'd be glad to lend a hand
with the clearing."
Uncle Al spoke at last. "No need.
I can manage."

Mr. DeHart and Mr. Salinas
looked at each other.
"We need your word on it, Al," Mr. DeHart said.
"If you need it, then you have it."
"We'll hold you to it," Mr. Salinas said.
Uncle Al clunked his cup
down hard on the table.
"I gave you my word."
"Good." Mr. DeHart pushed up his glasses.
"That's fine, Al. Just fine."

Then Mr. DeHart smiled at Eckhart.
"Why don't you come over and meet Eva
while you're visiting?"
"I'm not visiting," Eckhart said quickly.
"I live here."
He glanced at his uncle and added,
"For now anyway."

The two men looked surprised.

"In that case," Mr. DeHart said,

"you'll see Eva at school."

"I'm not going to school," Eckhart said.

Mr. DeHart raised his eyebrows.

"Not . . . going to school?"

He looked at Uncle Al.

"The boy needs to get his strength back,"

Uncle Al explained. "Been ill."

"Ah," said Mr. DeHart.


Another silence followed

as the two men waited

for some further explanation.

Eckhart hoped

Uncle Al might talk about the trial,

but he said only,

"The boy's parents died.

He had no place else to go."


"I always suspected," Mr. DeHart said,

"that you had a good heart underneath, Al."

"Don't tell anyone," Uncle Al said.

Laughing now,

Mr. Salinas and Mr. DeHart put on their coats.

"Thanks for the coffee," Mr. Salinas said,

winding his green muffler around his neck.

"Good-bye, Al," Mr. DeHart said.

"A pleasure meeting you, Eckhart."

Eckhart dipped his head.

After the men left,
Uncle Al walked to the window
and looked out
at the dead orchard.

"We've got a lot of work to do,
starting tomorrow."

Eckhart didn't like the sound of this.

"What kind of . . . work?" he asked.

Uncle Al turned. "You heard them.

All those dead trees
have to be cleared and burned by spring."

Eckhart's eyes widened.

"What, all of them?"

Uncle Al nodded. "I gave them my word."

## Chapter Twelve

That night
when Eckhart pulled the violin case
out from under his bed,
dirt smeared his fingers.
He dampened a washcloth
and cleaned every inch of the case.
He didn't open it—
hadn't opened it
since the accident.
Eckhart knew he should take the violin out
and play it.
Instruments needed to be played
to stay in good condition.

His mom had begun his violin lessons
when he was six.
Eckhart missed those lessons now,
missed music,

almost as much as he missed his mom.
Their last lesson together
had been a celebration.
His mom had picked up her violin
and said softly,
"Nobody can take this baby
away from me now."
For years she had rented the old violin,
but Eckhart's grandfather had died,
leaving her the money to buy it.
"Thanks, Dad," she added.
"I will now play Bach's Chaconne
just for you."

Standing before the open window,
she lifted her bow
like a wand of light
and began to play.
The old violin had a golden tone—
each note as bright and warm
as the sunshine
coming through the window.
Eckhart knew the Chaconne
from Bach's Partita in D Minor
was her favorite piece of music.
He liked it too—

the crashing chords,
the bright wildness,
the defiance
that made him feel
as though he would never be defeated.

After the last note faded,
his mom took a deep breath.
"That is the cry
of a shining soul
as it rises"—
she pointed her bow upward—
"fighting its way toward heaven."

Now, in his room,
crouched over the violin case,
Eckhart wondered if he would
ever
play the violin
ever
again.
A bit of the Chaconne
played through his head.
His mom had set words to part of the melody—
a special song
she had written just for him.

No.

He slid the case back under the bed
and stood up,
but the song still played in his mind,
the notes shifting
into the roar of a river.

Stop.

Eckhart took out his iPod,
and chose the Presto Finale
of Beethoven's Kreutzer Violin Sonata
for its speed and energy.
He switched on his 3DS
and started battling
the grisly Black Hand
in The Green Knight.
Here was something he could conquer—
a place where he could be a hero,
a world where if he made a mistake,
even a terrible one,
he could change it.

Eckhart played until he fell asleep.

Much later
the Black Hand squeezed Eckhart's throat,
roaring,
*You can't change it,*
*can't*
*ever*
*ever*
*change it. . . .*
Then Uncle Al was shaking him awake.
Trembling, Eckhart sat up.
Uncle Al didn't say a word,
but he left the light on.

Eckhart turned on the 3DS
and the Kreutzer Sonata again.
He fought
to stop the Black Hand
from extinguishing the candle—
fought
to pull the sword from the dead tree—
fought
to change it.

The next morning,
a Saturday,
Uncle Al insisted

that Eckhart take his morning tramp
on snowshoes
before they began clearing the orchard.
Uncle Al led him to a gate
in the west side of the deer fence.
Beyond the gate
an old road made a scar in the snow.
"That's Stagecoach Road," Uncle Al said.
"Go south, and it climbs Stagecoach Hill."
He pointed. "But go north,
over that smaller hill there,
and the road drops into the canyon
behind the DeHarts' orchard.
There's a lot to see in the canyon."

Eckhart stared through the wire,
scared to go outside the deer fence.
Uncle Al had said
the coyotes weren't dangerous,
but what about cougars or bears?
Once, Sir Gawain had faced wild beasts
in an enchanted forest.
He had charged straight into them
without hesitating.
So when Uncle Al opened the gate,
Eckhart squared his shoulders

and stepped through.

He headed north
on Stagecoach Road
because the hill there was smaller.
Even so, the hike up
through the green and gray bushes
prickling from the snow
left him hot and panting for breath.
He unzipped his coat.
Snowshoeing down the other side
of the hill was fun, though,
and Eckhart soon found himself
in a canyon between the hills.
Here and there, pine trees stood
like green sentinels,
towering over the aspen trees
with their white and black bark.
An aspen had grown
in his backyard at home.

But the canyon was nothing like home.

Creature tracks
etched the snow—
some sharp,

some delicate and twiggy,
others round like dog prints.
Eckhart thought of the coyotes
and glanced nervously
back over his shoulder.
Only the wind moved,
tossing showers of snow
down from the trees.

A snowy path
crisscrossed with ski tracks
threaded the bottom of the canyon.
Sloping upward,
the ground rose
toward a low mountain in the west.
Eckhart tramped up the path.
Suddenly he stopped and listened,
but heard only silence—
no river,
no roaring.
He took a deep breath.

Then a hissing sound
came from somewhere ahead.
A wild animal?
Eckhart's heart pounded.

He saw a flash of white
as a girl in a white jacket flew
around the bend on skis,
her hair streaming out behind her.
"Watch out!" he cried.
She veered,
but it was too late.
She crashed into him,
and together
they tumbled into the snow.

## Chapter Thirteen

Lying on his back,
staring up at a blue sky
laced with white branches,
Eckhart heard a merry laugh.
"Are you all right?" the girl asked,
sitting beside him in the snow.
Eckhart sat up cautiously. "I think so."
As quick and graceful as a dancer,
the girl pushed herself up
from the ground
and back onto her skis.
"Sorry I crashed into you," she said,
holding out her hand.
"That's all right," Eckhart mumbled.
He didn't take her hand,
but clambered to his feet
and looked at her.

Looking intently back
was the girl in the shining silver boots.


"Why," she said,
"you look like an Eckhart."
Seeing his surprise,
she added, "My dad told me about you."
Her eyes were green,
her cheeks bubble-gum pink.
She wore a blue hat
pulled low on her head.
"I'm Eva," she said, "Eva DeHart.
Poet and so-so skier.
Do you ski, Eckhart?"
"No."
"Oh, you should!" she exclaimed.
"It's much more fun
than snowshoeing.
Like flying
when you're coming down the canyon.
I was imagining I was Melora
in her disguise
as the Knight of the Blue Surcoat,
riding at the head
of the army of Babylon."

Eckhart looked at her, astounded.

"You mean Melora,

King Arthur's daughter?"

"Yes." Eva swung one ski pole.

"You've heard of her?"

Eckhart nodded. "I've read everything

I can find about the Round Table."

"Me too!" she cried. "Who do you think

was the bravest of Arthur's knights?"

"Sir Gawain," Eckhart said.

"Yes," she agreed. "He was brave—

facing the Green Knight

to save his uncle the king's life."


A breeze blew by.

Eckhart hunched his shoulders,

cold from standing still.

Eva noticed. "Are you going up or down?

If you're going down,

I'll go with you."

"Down," Eckhart said at once.

They started back down the path,

Eva skiing slowly,

poking her poles into the snow.


Eckhart asked, "Do you know

what all these animal tracks are?"

"Most of them," she said.

Eckhart looked all around.

"Are there dangerous animals
in the canyon?"

Her face turned serious.

"I saw a bear once,
but it only ran away.
I've never seen a cougar,
though I've spotted their tracks.
And in summer you sometimes see rattlers,
though your uncle
keeps the den cleared out."

"The den?" Eckhart asked.

"There's a rattlesnake den
on that rocky hill south of your orchard.
We call it Rattler Hill.
Your uncle clears it out every year.
Except," she added softly,
"the year that Lily died."

Lily.
Eckhart thought of the picture in his room,
and the four peach trees
growing by the hill near the house.
"How did Lily die?" he asked.

Sliding her skis to one side,
Eva looked at him in surprise.
"You don't know?"
Eckhart shook his head.
"My mom never said much
about my uncle.
They didn't get along."
Eva leaned on one pole.
"It happened three years ago.
Lily was seven. A rattlesnake bit her.
You can survive that,
but by the time they found her,
it was too late."

Eckhart was silent for a moment,
then asked, "What was Lily like?"
"She was . . ." Eva tipped her head, thinking.
"Like a fairy. She laughed a lot.
And she had a bracelet of white beads
that she called pearls.
She gave it to me on my ninth birthday.
After she died,
I scattered some of the beads up here."
Eva glanced around.
"That's when the canyon
first turned magical for me.

Sometimes I imagine
I hear her laughing."

Eckhart looked around the canyon—
at the pine trees,
at the mysterious tracks in the snow,
at the brush,
at the hills,
at the low mountain rising to the west,
and finally at Eva.

She smiled at him—
a smile so sweet,
so bright,
so warm,
that suddenly Eckhart felt his heart
unclench.
"After all," she said,
"with Lily laughing in the canyon,
how couldn't it be magic?"

# Chapter Fourteen

Later that day,
kneeling in the snow
in the dead orchard,
Eckhart wrapped a heavy chain
around a stump.
He struggled to hook it tight
as his uncle had shown him,
but the work gloves he wore
made his fingers
clumsy and slow.

The other end of the chain
was fastened to the tractor
chugging behind him.
With all his strength
Eckhart pulled and pulled
and at last
hooked the chain around the stump.

Straightening, he stepped back
and waved to Uncle Al.

Uncle Al put the tractor in gear
and drove it away from the stump.
The chain tightened—
metal groaning against wood—
but the stump clung to the earth.
As the tractor wheels began to spin,
the stubborn stump wrenched
from the ground.
The roots,
pulled from the darkness,
scrabbled in the air and light.

Eckhart unhooked the chain,
and Uncle Al drove the tractor
toward the next stump.
They had been working
for only an hour,
but already Eckhart felt
like he had been pulling stumps forever.
He looked at the row
of uprooted stumps behind him—
maybe a dozen?
And there were, what,

maybe eighty more stumps
to pull out in this row alone?
Then he stared at all the rows and rows ahead.
Fifty? Sixty?
And each with a hundred trees.
That made five or six thousand stumps!

The task seemed impossible,
unless he were a wizard or Hercules.
With the tractor in position,
Uncle Al waved at him
to hook the chain
around the next stump.
Tired,
resentful,
Eckhart trudged forward.
He hated this—
hated the cold,
hated the boredom,
hated the tussling with the chain,
hated the stupid gloves.

Then the ever present roar
of the river
caught his attention.
Maybe this is the trial, he told himself.

After all, he had wanted the trial to be hard.

And he wanted to prove himself

to Uncle Al.

Eckhart thought of Sir Gawain.

He also had needed to prove

his worth to his uncle, King Arthur.

Only after Sir Gawain had rescued

the lady in the Castle of Maidens

had the king acknowledged

Gawain as his nephew.

Eckhart sighed

as he hooked the chain

around the stump.

Sir Gawain's trial was a lot more interesting

than mine, he thought.

But he was afraid to complain—

Uncle Al might send him away.

Sunrise Orchard might not be the home

Eckhart wanted,

but it was better than no home at all.

While the tractor dragged

out the stump,

Eckhart looked up at Rattler Hill.

Dark gray rocks nosed

through the snow

like silent, sleeping beasts.

Now, in winter,
the rattlers would be hibernating
deep in their rocky den.
Eckhart wished he had met Lily,
had heard her laugh.
He knew his mom and uncle
had disliked each other,
but that seemed like a poor reason
to have kept him from his only cousin.
And now it was too late—
for so many things.

*Too late* . . . ,
the river roared.
*Too late*. . . .

Uncle Al waved him forward,
and Eckhart trudged
toward the next stump.

After what seemed like forever
but was really only three hours,
Uncle All yelled, "That's enough."
He zigzagged the tractor
between the tumbled stumps
and drove up the road toward the shop.

Eckhart—
his back aching,
his hands sore—
watched the weak winter sunlight
gleam on the uprooted stumps.
They had pulled maybe one tenth
of the stumps in the orchard,
if even that.
He thought of the long,
boring
days ahead
and wanted to scream.

That night,
even though Eckhart was so tired
he could hardly keep his eyes open,
he started The Green Knight.
Inside the Chapel Perilous
he stumbled into a new room,
where twisting tree roots dangled
from a dirt ceiling.

Tucked into one root,
glowing moon-bright,
was a pearl.
Eckhart seized it.

He fought his way back
to the sword
stuck in the dead tree.
When he slipped the pearl
into the notch on the golden hilt,
the sword flashed.
Grasping the hilt,
Eckhart pulled the sword
out of the dead tree.

At last!

Smiling,
Eckhart turned off the 3DS.
He yawned
and looked out the round window.
Moonlight powdered
the tops of the pine trees
winding up the canyon—
ponderosa pines, Eva had called them.
Up in the canyon
were beads of secret laughter.
Up in the canyon
was a girl with a bright smile
who talked about magic.

Maybe it wasn't too late.

He lay down.
And for the first time since Hell's Canyon,
Eckhart fell asleep
as soon as he pulled up the covers—
no howling,
no roaring river,
no nightmares,
no faces in the water,
no Black Hand
disturbed his sleep.

## Chapter Fifteen

Eckhart's days at Sunrise Orchard
fell into a rhythm.
After breakfast—
pancakes, French toast, or oatmeal—
Uncle Al insisted that Eckhart
spend an hour
tramping around on snowshoes.
Then they spent three hours
pulling stumps in the orchard.
After lunch Eckhart worked
in his schoolbooks for three hours.
In the evenings he gamed or read.
After a week of this routine,
his muscles stopped aching.
He even looked forward
to his morning tramp on snowshoes
because it was so much better
than pulling stumps.

Uncle Al still hadn't said one word
about the trial.

Late one afternoon,
after two weeks at Sunrise Orchard,
Eckhart didn't know what else to do,
so he explored the second floor
of the shop building.
Back home
he'd never had enough free time.
Each hour in each day
had its scheduled purpose—
hours
for school and homework,
hours
for violin practice,
hours
for meals, chores, and family outings.
Now, Eckhart thought,
opening a door in the shop,
I have too much free time.
He didn't know what to do with it.

The first room was packed
with hunting and fishing equipment—
duck decoys, life jackets,

fishing poles, and tackle boxes.
The second room had woodworking tools—
a lathe, a band saw, a table saw,
and other tools covered with dust.

Eckhart's dad,
a mechanical engineer,
had dabbled in a woodworking shop
in their garage.
Time and time again
he had offered to teach Eckhart
to use the tools,
but Eckhart had always been too busy.
"My best jokes come to me out here,"
his dad had told him. "Like this one:
Did you hear about the shoe sale?"
"No," Eckhart said.
His dad grinned. "Buy two, get one free."
Eckhart frowned. "I don't get it."
"One shoe," his dad explained.
"What do you do with one shoe?"
Groaning, Eckhart laughed.

Now, running his finger
over Uncle Al's lathe,
Eckhart knew he would give anything—

anything at all—
to have his dad standing here,
right now,
cracking bad jokes
and teaching him about the lathe.
Then rage crackled through him.
"Why, Dad?
Why did you make us go rafting?
Why did you jump in after Mom?
If you hadn't . . .
you'd still be here."

Eckhart turned sharply
away from the lathe.
Then he saw something
that made his breath catch.
In the corner,
in a shaft of sunlight,
an oak chair gleamed a soft, warm gold.
Not one speck of dust
lay on the ornate arms and legs.
A sunburst carved on the back
sent out long, curling rays.
Eckhart traced them with his fingers.
The wood, perfectly sanded and polished,
felt as smooth as satin.

It was a chair fit for a knight.
Eckhart carried the chair
down the steps,
out of the shop building,
through the patches of remaining snow,
and around the blue spruce trees.
Climbing the deck stairs,
he thought of the Siege Perilous—
the chair at Arthur's Round Table
reserved for the knight
who achieved the quest
of the Holy Grail.
Anyone else who sat in that chair
would die.

Inside the house
Eckhart pushed the crate away
and set the chair in its place.
He admired it for a moment,
then sat down to try it out.
His legs didn't quite reach the floor.

Uncle Al came into the house,
saw him in the chair,
and stopped dead.
"What do you think you're doing?"

Eckhart explained, "I found this in the—"
"Get out of that chair!" Uncle Al's face was white.
"But—"
"Get out of that chair. Now."
Eckhart jumped up.
Uncle Al grabbed the chair
and started toward the door.

Eckhart blurted, "But why can't I have it?
I hate sitting on a crate.
No one was using that chair."
Uncle Al turned. "You can't just take
anything you want.
This isn't your house."

As Eckhart glared at Uncle Al,
something hurt—
something frightened—
something angry—
something clinging to a log in rushing water—
came roaring out of him.
"Not my house?" he shouted. "Why not?
I'm pulling out all those stupid stumps.
I'm sick of this stupid trial—
sick of it!
I don't even know what I have to do

to make this my house,
because you won't tell me!"

Uncle Al wrapped his arms
around the chair.
"This was Lily's chair.
I made it for her. For Lily.
Not you." He turned away.
"You'll spend the rest of the day
all by yourself in your room."
And he opened the door.

Eckhart choked back a sob.
"But I'm already all by myself.
All the time.
I've been all by myself
since I fell . . .
in the river."
He swallowed hard. "I didn't know . . .
what to do.
I couldn't—
the water was—
I was so scared. . . .
And they died."
Eckhart stood,
trembling.

He felt small—
as small as a pebble
at the bottom of the sea.
"I'm all by myself," he said again.

A cold wind blew through the open door.
Uncle Al set Lily's chair
down on the threshold.
He grasped the back of the chair,
his fingers fitting
into the sunburst's curling rays.
"Lily was all by herself too," he said,
"when she died."
Eckhart looked at him.
His uncle looked steadily back—
the usual hard glint in his eyes
had softened.
"Tell me," Uncle Al said quietly.
"Tell me what happened on the river."

Eckhart opened his mouth,
then closed it again.
"I couldn't . . . ," he began.
"Couldn't—"
He stopped.
"You can tell me," Uncle Al said.

His eyes are like Mom's, Eckhart thought.
Blue, like . . . kindness.
Then something inside him—
a dam of grief
and guilt
and horror—
rocked
and shook
and finally broke
as the nightmare
of Hell's Canyon
came rushing out of him.

## Chapter Sixteen

The raft they rode
down the Snake River
was the color of Tang.
So were the life jackets
strapped to Eckhart,
his parents, and their guide.
Cliffs scorched
with the colors of rose and gold
reared up,
making a gorge for the jade river—
one of the deepest gorges
in North America.
The narrow sky
at the top of the gorge
shone a brilliant blue.

Each time the raft
bumped and bucked
over a rapid,

Eckhart closed his eyes.
But to his surprise
he found that he didn't hate
this ride down the river.
He saw things—
the Seven Devils range striding to the east,
a herd of bighorn sheep grazing on a hill,
a peregrine falcon sailing overhead.

His mom,
perched on the other side of the raft,
grinned at him.
His dad,
sitting ahead,
paddled hard.
We'll all be sore tomorrow, Eckhart thought.
But he found himself smiling.
He watched
the seeds twirling on the wind
land on the water,
where the current spun them away
in a helpless dance.

Then the roaring
grew louder and louder
until it was all he could hear,

until it was the only thing in the world.
Was it the big rapid,
was it Wild Goose?
Their guide had warned them
to stay sharp
when they hit Wild Goose.
So this time Eckhart kept his eyes open
as the raft rippled
over the rocks
like a roller coaster
that was wild and alive.
When the spray arched up
and splashed his face,
Eckhart laughed.

The guide screamed.

The raft slammed
against a boulder
and shot straight up.
Eckhart plunged into the water.
Buoyed by the life jacket,
he popped up again.
His arms flailed in the current
as it swept him forward,
relentlessly forward.

Eckhart fought
to keep his legs in front of him,
as the guide had told them,
but the current danced him
like a puppet
as he slammed
and spun
from rock to rock.

White spray
surrounded him,
blinded him,
severed him
from the world.
"Mom!" he screamed. "Dad!"
But the thundering river
swallowed his screams.

He was alone.

A log reared out of the water.
Eckhart twisted,
kicked—
reached—
grabbed—
and hooked his arms over the log.

The river dragged
his legs underneath,
but Eckhart hung on.

It took all his strength.

He looked for the shore,
but saw only the river
churning against steep canyon walls.
Then, not ten feet away,
Eckhart's dad crawled
out of the water onto a boulder.
"Dad!" Eckhart shouted.
Then his mom,
tumbled by the current,
came shooting toward him.
"Mom!" Eckhart yelled.
Fear clenched her face.
"Grab her, Eckhart!" his dad shouted.
"Reach! Give her your hand!"

Eckhart's heart pounded in his ears,
a drum over the roar of the river.
He wanted to get her—
he tried to get her—
even lifted one hand from the log.

But as soon as he did,
the current nearly
dragged him under.
"Eckhart, no!" his mom screamed.
"Hold on!"

Eckhart slapped his hand back on the log.

His mom swirled by,
close,
so close,
her hair streaming out.
"Eckhart!" his dad shouted. "Save her!"
But Eckhart found that his hand
would not
let go
of the log.
His mom swept past him
and vanished under the logjam ahead.
"Rose!" his dad screamed.
He jumped off the boulder
into the river,
which flung him
under the logjam too.

Neither of them came up again.

## Chapter Seventeen

When Eckhart finished
telling his uncle
what had happened on the river,
Uncle Al didn't say a word.
He was still
leaning on Lily's golden chair,
and the front door still
stood open,
letting in the freezing wind.

Shaking from the cold,
from the shock of the telling,
Eckhart couldn't look at his uncle.
He felt shriveled,
filthy—
like something unwanted
in the corner of a dank basement,
something even the rats disdained.

His eyes fixed on the sunburst
on the back of the chair.
He wanted sun.
Wanted warmth.
Wanted music.
Wanted his parents back.
"If I had let go," he said,
his shoulders sagging,
"if I had reached out like Dad said—
I might have saved her."

Uncle Al spoke at last.
"You don't know that.
It's just as likely
that you would have been swept away
and drowned too.
Rose wouldn't have wanted that,
believe me."
"I'll never know," Eckhart said.
He wrapped his arms around himself,
against cold,
against anguish.

Uncle Al slid Lily's chair into the house
and shut the door.
"Lily was near the hammock," he said,

"when the rattler bit her.
I thought she'd gone to town
with her mother.
I was working in the orchard,
fighting fire blight.
There was so much to do,
I hadn't got around
to clearing out the den on Rattler Hill.
If I had . . ."
He looked at Eckhart,
and then shook his head.
"I'll never know.
Like you."

Eckhart stood in surprise.
He had thought Uncle Al
would end the trial,
would send him away
now that he knew the horrible truth.
Instead Uncle Al seemed to understand.
"I wish . . . ," Eckhart began.
"I can't change it, ever, I know.
But I wish there was something . . ."
He shook his head miserably.
"I don't know what."

Uncle Al took a deep breath,
and his hands tightened on Lily's chair.
"I took you in," he said,
"to make up for . . .
what happened to Lily.
I can't change
what happened to her either,
but it's a way to make things right."
He looked at Eckhart.
"Maybe you need to find a way
to make things right too."
And, taking Lily's chair,
Uncle Al went out the door.

Eckhart stood for a moment,
rubbing his cold arms.
Then he saw the sheepskin
on the back of the limping couch.
"Mom," he whispered.
He walked over
and dug his fingers into the fleece.
"By my troth, Mom," he said,
"I'll find a way to make things right."
And, lifting the sheepskin,
he wrapped himself
in its wooly warmth.

PART 2:

The Tower of Troth

## Chapter Eighteen

Eckhart walked along Stagecoach Road
to the canyon behind Eva's place,
without wearing snowshoes.
Three weeks had passed,
and now, near the end of March,
all the deep snow had melted,
leaving only scattered drifts of white
on the ground.
He had been at Sunrise Orchard
for five weeks.

Winding between the aspens and pines,
Eckhart passed the spot
where Eva had crashed into him
on her skis.
He went on up the path
beside the creek.
The trickling water—

so bright, so bubbly—
sounded like laughter,
and he thought of Lily.

After a quarter of a mile,
the trees stopped,
and the path opened into a meadow.
There, beside the creek,
big rocks formed a rectangle on the ground.
Eckhart was studying them,
wondering what they might be,
when the bushes crackled.

He looked up.
Something big and black
bounded straight toward him.
His heart jumped.
Then he saw it was only a dog,
not a bear,
not a cougar—
just a plain old black Lab.
He sighed with relief.

Not far behind the dog
Eva ran toward him
in her shining silver boots.

They sparkled in the sunlight.

"Sirius," she called,

as the dog leaped against Eckhart. "Get down!"

Eckhart patted the dog's head.

"His name is Sirius?"

Eva laughed. "Yes.

And my brother's name is Achilles.

And my name is really Evangeline."

Seeing his blank look, she added,

"Evangeline's a heroine

in an old poem.

My mom loves poetry

and Greek mythology."

"Cool," said Eckhart.

He pointed to the rectangle of stones.

"What are those for?"

"They're foundation stones," Eva explained,

"all that's left of an old homestead."

After stepping onto the stones,

she leaped from one to the other

all the way around the foundation.

It didn't take long.

"Not a very big house," Eckhart said.

"Who lived in it?"

"I don't know," Eva said.

"But I like to think of it
as a monument to the pioneers.
Sometimes I lay flowers here
in their memory."

Eckhart liked that.
Then a thought pushed into his mind.
His parents had no monument—
no graves that he might visit
and lay flowers on.
They had been cremated,
their ashes scattered over Puget Sound.
He turned away
so Eva would not see
him blinking hard.

Eva said, "I put one of Lily's 'pearls'
under one of these stones."
She jumped down and asked,
"Do you want to see my Chapel Perilous?"
Eckhart stared in surprise.
"You mean, like the Chapel Perilous
in King Arthur?"
Eva nodded. "I made one of my own.
Everyone ought to have one,
don't you think?"

She grinned.

Eckhart pictured the grisly Black Hand

in The Green Knight.

"I don't know," he said slowly.

"The Chapel Perilous was a dangerous place."

Eva nodded. "Yes, most crossroads

and places of magical aid

can be dangerous,

but that's because they challenge you

to be more than you are."

Eckhart thought about that.

He opened his mouth to tell her

about the game,

then stopped.

The game was something

he wanted to keep to himself.

"You must swear on your honor," Eva said,

"that you will never ever

reveal the chapel's location."

"By my troth," Eckhart said solemnly.

Eva beamed.

"Gramercy!" she exclaimed.

That, Eckhart knew,

was how people in King Arthur's time

expressed thanks, wonder, or surprise.
"Come on," Eva cried,
and she started across the meadow.

When they reached the creek,
they climbed down a small gully.
Eva almost flew across the water,
hopping from rock to rock,
but Eckhart stepped cautiously.
On the other side of the creek,
they climbed up the steep bank
into the bushes.

Eckhart had learned
that the silvery-green bushes
were called sagebrush.
They smelled like the herb
his dad had mixed into the stuffing
on Thanksgiving.
The yellow-green bushes
were called bitterbrush.
Sagebrush and bitterbrush
grew not only in the meadow
but rioted all across the hills.

Eckhart and Eva soon reached

the north side of the canyon.
Eckhart saw a rocky outcrop
in the side of the hill,
with a screen of woven pine boughs
hanging across it.
Hanging from the boughs were
bird skulls,
antlers,
backbones—
all bleached white from the sun.
"Behold," Eva said. "The Chapel Perilous.
Wait here, Sirius."
And, lifting the screen,
she ducked inside.

Eckhart stood outside for a moment,
looking at the bones.
Then, taking a deep breath,
he followed her in.

## Chapter Nineteen

Eva's Chapel Perilous
was a shallow cave
with stone walls on three sides.
In the center,
on a crate covered with a golden cloth,
stood a white candle.
"This is the altar," Eva said to Eckhart.
"Every chapel must have its altar."
A circle of polished stones
surrounded the candle.
At the back of the altar
lay a bouquet of dried golden daisies.
Eva pointed to a log.
"That's the pew for us supplicants to sit on."
Eckhart sat down.
She pulled a book of matches
from her pocket
and lit the candle.

Eckhart half expected the Black Hand
to creep out
from some crevice in the rock.
Instead, in the flickering light,
pictures came alive on the walls—
a unicorn with a shining horn,
a dragon with its wings outstretched,
a garland of leaves, apples, and flowers.
Amazed, Eckhart asked,
"Did you paint all this?"
"No. My best friend, Chloe, did,
before she moved away."
Eva sighed. "After Chloe left,
I didn't come here for a long time.
It made me miss her too much."

"What do you do in here?" he asked.
"I think about crossroads.
About which way to turn . . .
what to do next.
And I call on magic to help me."
Eckhart watched the candlelight dance
across the unicorn's mane.
"Do you really believe in magic?" he asked.
Eva looked at him seriously.
"I believe in the Greater Power of Imagination.

I know it can help you
find your heart's desire."

A silence followed—
not a lonely silence, a good one,
like the gathering of breath
before a song.
"What is your heart's desire?" Eckhart asked.
Eva tipped her head.
"Now that we get to keep the Farm—
we almost lost it, you know—
my heart's desire is to find a new best friend."
She paused, then asked,
"What is your heart's desire?"
"I want . . ." Eckhart stopped.
"Two things, really.
First I want a home."
Eva raised her eyebrows.
"But don't you have a home here
with your uncle?"
Eckhart sighed. "Only on trial."

"Oh," Eva said softly,
a strange expression on her face.
"Oh, I didn't know that."
A breeze wandered into the cave,

clicking the bones on the screen.
As the candle flame swayed,
Eckhart thought again
of the Black Hand
trying to snuff out the candle.
Eva asked, "What are the tests for the trial?"
"That's just the problem!" he exclaimed.
"I don't know."
Eva frowned. "That does makes it hard.
So what's the other thing your heart desires?"

Eckhart searched for the right words.
"I want to prove . . . ," he began.
"I mean, I want to be courageous.
To prove I'm not a coward.
There's something"—
he looked up at her suddenly,
desperately—
"something terrible I must make up for."

Eckhart bit his lip
and wished he could grab the words back.
She might make fun of him,
might ask questions he didn't want to answer.
But to his surprise
Eva merely nodded. "Two worthy desires.

You are on a quest, then,
for home and for courage."

"Yes," Eckhart said slowly.
"Yes, that's true."
He picked up a polished blue rock
from the altar and sighed.
"But I don't know how to get them."
Eva cupped her chin in her hand.
"Well, most knights who set out
on their quests don't know how
they're going to achieve them.
The important thing is to set out."
Nodding, Eckhart spoke his agreement
as people did in King Arthur's time—
"I assent me."

"But," Eva added, "before you can set out,
you must face your fears.
So let's call upon
magical aid to help you."
"How?" he asked.
Eva held up her arms
and faced the altar.
"Repeat after me," she said.
"I call on the spirit of stone,

that I may be as strong as you."
Eckhart repeated it.
"I call on the leaping greenly spirits of the trees
—that's from a poem—
that I may be rooted and wise."
Eckhart repeated it.
"I call on the sun,
that it may shine on my path."
Eckhart repeated it.
"I call on the water,
that it may cleanse me."

Eckhart did not repeat this.
Eva glanced at him, then went on.
"Earth, Fire, Water, and Air,
show Eckhart the way from the crossroads.
In God we trust. Amen."
Eva lowered her arms
and looked at Eckhart with shining eyes.
"Your name is Eckhart Lyon.
You shall become Eckhart, Lion Heart."

As Eckhart stared at her,
he felt something
rise,
something he had not felt in months

rise
from a place long dark and sore—
and with it came a sudden glimmer
like sunlight on a bird's wing.

It was hope.

## Chapter Twenty

When Eckhart arrived
back at the house,
he stamped the canyon dirt off his boots.
He was reaching for the doorknob,
when he noticed the hatchet and wood block.
*You must face your fears*, Eva had said.

Eckhart set a log on the block
and picked up the hatchet.
The sharp edge gleamed.
Taking a deep breath,
Eckhart raised the hatchet,
hesitated,
then swung it down slowly—
barely nicking the wood.
He tried again.
This time he swung the hatchet too fast
and, afraid for his fingers,

let go of the log.
It clattered onto the deck.
Gritting his teeth,
Eckhart picked up the log
and tried a third time,
swinging gently but firmly.
The blade bit into the wood.
He tapped the log and hatchet together
against the wood block
as Uncle Al had shown him,
and a sliver of wood split
off from the log.

Astonished by his success,
Eckhart held up the stick of kindling
and grinned.
Again and again
he swung the hatchet,
and the river seemed merely to mumble
in the distance,
instead of roar.

When Uncle Al came in later,
he noticed the crate stuffed with kindling.
He looked surprised
but didn't say a word.

At eleven o'clock the next morning,
they pulled the last stump
from the dead orchard.
Eckhart looked across the field
at the mess of stumps, brush, and branches.
"What now?" he asked Uncle Al.
"Now we put the blade on the tractor
and push all the brush into piles.
Then we burn it."
Eckhart blinked. "Burn all that?"
His brain tried to calculate
how long it would take
to burn all the brush
in the woodstove.

"Bonfires," Uncle Al said,
as though reading Eckhart's mind.
"Time you learned to drive the tractor."
"Me?" Eckhart's voice squeaked.
"Me . . . drive that thing?"
"Yes, you. Get on."

Eckhart stared at the tractor.
It was huge,
with two enormous wheels in back
and two smaller wheels in front.

Dials plastered the dashboard
liked goggling eyes.
Gear shifts sprouted upward,
and hoses sprang out like tentacles.
It looked like a big green monster.
Eckhart didn't want to get on it—
not one bit.
Then he thought of Sir Gawain.
What would Gawain do?
He had faced the Green Knight
and the monstrous giant Gormundus.
Wasn't the tractor
really a kind of green Gormundus?
*Face your fears,*
Eva's voice whispered in his mind.
And Uncle Al was waiting.
So Eckhart took a deep breath
and climbed up
onto the tractor seat.

Two hours later
he was driving the tractor
through the dead orchard
pushing brush and stumps into piles.
Uncle Al had told him to make
six big brush piles.

Eckhart grinned as he shifted gears.
He couldn't believe
he was operating a tractor,
doing it well,
and having fun, too.
This was almost as exciting
as gaming on his 3DS.
He was commanding powerful forces,
ridding the world of dead zombie trees!

That night,
playing The Green Knight in bed,
Eckhart at last unearthed his helm
from the bones of a wasteland.
Now, armed with sword
and spear
and helm,
he would finally be able to stop
the Black Hand
from snuffing out the candle.

But then the game changed—
a new objective showed,
and Eckhart realized he needed something more.
He saw something white,
floating . . .

and after it he went.
Faster and faster he played,
as though his life depended on winning.
Then the Black Hand pounced—
the candle went out,
and Eckhart fell
in a shower of branches,
fell
and fell—
down
into darkness.

It took three days
to gather all the brush into piles.
On the fourth day,
Uncle Al poured gas
on two of the brush piles
and set them on fire.
As a precaution, the sprayer,
a machine that sprayed pesticides on fruit,
was standing nearby
filled with water.
Eckhart watched
the flames leap up the brush,
devouring the dead wood

as it crackled and snapped.
Smoke curled up,
blown north by the wind.
Uncle Al stood watching too.

"Why," Eckhart asked,
"did you cut down the orchard three years ago?"
Uncle Al didn't say anything,
and for a moment
Eckhart thought he wouldn't answer.
"Mostly because of fire blight," he said at last.
"It killed three quarters of the trees
the summer Lily died.
After . . . I cut out the rest
because I was out here working
when she was bit.
I couldn't look at the trees.
If it weren't for the damned orchard . . ."
He stopped.

"What happened to Lily's mom," Eckhart asked,
"my aunt Irina?"
Uncle Al leaned against the sprayer
and crossed his arms.
"She left me after Lily died.

After I cut down the orchard.
We couldn't bear . . .
We're separated now."
His eyes hardened.
"Never trust a woman.
All they do is leave you."

## Chapter Twenty-One

April began
with sun-drenched skies
and only a few days
of spitting, dancing snow—
as though winter
couldn't quite bear to let go.
The graveyard of trees was gone.
Eckhart's heart lifted
every time he looked
over the clean, empty field.

He went over to Eva's house
a few times,
but she was always busy,
so he stopped trying.
When he chanced to meet her
in the canyon, though,
she seemed friendly enough.

She showed him all the special places—
the abandoned mines in the hills,
the rise beyond the second meadow
where you could often spot deer,
and the old wheat flat above the canyon,
now covered with sagebrush.
Up on the flat
they could walk for miles.
And they could see forever—
north toward the town of Twisp,
south toward Billy Goat Mountain,
and west toward Heaven's Gate Mountain,
where snow still lingered.

Sometimes,
on fine afternoons,
Eckhart went shed hunting
with Uncle Al and Cub.
Sheds, Eckhart knew now,
were what you called a buck's antlers
after he shed them in the winter.
He and Uncle Al would walk up
Black Canyon Creek to the south
or Libby Creek to the north,
searching for sheds.

Whenever Cub found one,
he stood over it
barking proudly.

Usually they walked in silence,
but one day,
as they were coming home
with two new sheds
to add to the antler trees,
Eckhart asked, "Do you celebrate Easter?"
"Sometimes," Uncle Al said. "You?"
Eckhart nodded. "Ham and eggs."
Uncle Al looked startled.
"You had breakfast for Easter?"
"No, that's just what my dad
always called Easter.
Because we always had ham for dinner
and always colored Easter eggs.
Dad would . . ." Eckhart stopped,
blinked hard,
and pretended to search the grass for sheds.

Uncle Al glanced at him.
"I've a hankering for turkey.
Didn't celebrate Thanksgiving this year—

or Christmas."
"Me either," Eckhart said softly.
His uncle nodded.
"Then turkey it is for Easter—
turkey and eggs."
Cub sniffed a pine tree ahead
and started barking.
Uncle Al said,
"He's found another one."

On Easter morning
Uncle Al stood shaking a jar
of poultry seasoning into the stuffing mix.
"Empty," he said.
"Should be another jar
in that high cupboard there."
Eckhart dragged his uncle's chair
across the kitchen,
stepped up,
and started rummaging
through the cupboard.

He found
a bag of brown sugar,
a bottle of brandy,

a bag of dates,
a box of spaghetti,
and a jar filled with something orange.
On the jar's label
the words "Lily's Peaches"
were written in crooked letters—
the same crooked letters
as those on the picture of the house
up in Eckhart's room.
He looked at it a moment,
then spotted the poultry seasoning
in the corner.


After handing the jar to his uncle,
Eckhart asked, "Will you tell me
about Lily's peach trees?"
The wooden spoon in Uncle Al's hand stopped
in midair.
His face grew still,
as though he were listening
to something far away.


"When Lily was four," Uncle Al began,
"she decided she wanted her own orchard.
She loved peaches and cherries.

After thinking it over
for about a minute,
she chose peaches
because she loved peach pie best."
Uncle Al squinted down at the bowl
and started mixing the stuffing again.
"So," he added, "I bought her
four little Red Haven peach trees."
He smiled,
and Eckhart thought it the sweetest,
saddest
smile he had ever seen.

His uncle went on.
"You should've seen Lily plant them.
She insisted on digging the holes herself—
there was more dirt on her
than on the ground.
And when a little peach
appeared the second year,
she picked it
and tried to bake a peach pie
in her Easy-Bake Oven."
Uncle Al laughed. "I had to eat it.
It was the best worst pie I ever ate."
He walked to the refrigerator.

Eckhart, watching him,
saw loneliness
in the curve of his uncle's back.

When the stuffing was ready,
Eckhart dropped spoonfuls
into the slippery turkey.
"It's full," he said.
But Uncle Al, holding the turkey open,
shook his head. "Pack it in.
Stuffing should be moist."
So Eckhart spooned in more.
"That's good," Uncle Al said.
He pulled the skin away from the neck.
"Put some under there."
"Under the skin?" Eckhart asked, surprised.
"Sure. The crop's the best place of all.
The stuffing soaks up all the fat."

Eckhart tried,
but the stuffing kept falling off the spoon.
"Use your hands," Uncle Al advised.
My hands? Eckhart thought.
His mom would never have allowed that—
she worried about germs.
"Best tool for the job," Uncle Al said.

So Eckhart scooped up a handful
of squishy stuffing from the bowl
and shoved it under the skin.
"More," Uncle Al said.
Eckhart slipped in another handful.
"Pack it in!" Uncle Al urged.
Grinning, Eckhart shoved in more stuffing.
"Come on!" Uncle Al exclaimed.
"Pack it in! Pack it in!"
"I am! I am!" Eckhart laughed,
his hands flying
from the bowl to the bird
until he was laughing so hard,
he could hardly stand up.
The bird looked like a lumpy mattress.

"Every Thanksgiving," Eckhart said,
"my dad told the same joke.
Why did the police arrest the turkey?"
"Couldn't say," Uncle Al said.
"Because," Eckhart said,
"they suspected fowl play."
Uncle Al groaned.
Eckhart grinned. "If the police
saw this lumpy turkey,
they'd think it was hiding stuff under its skin.

Get it? Stuff—stuffing!"
Uncle Al shook his head. "Just wait
until you taste it."

When the turkey was cooked,
when the salad was tossed,
when the table was set,
they sat down together to eat.
Eckhart glanced at the bowl
of colored Easter eggs he had made
while the turkey was cooking.
Even though he was too old for Easter eggs,
it had been fun.
Something caught his eye.
Someone had glued twigs
onto one of the eggs—
like antlers.

Eckhart glanced at his uncle,
smiled,
and took a bite of the stuffing
scooped from the crop.
He tasted raisins,
chestnuts,
walnuts,
butter—

a burst of sweet and salt and fat
that was nothing like the stuffing
his parents had made.
Eckhart looked at his uncle.
"You're right," he said.
"The crop's the best."

## Chapter Twenty-Two

At the end of April
the land woke up,
singing a song of color.
Golden sun daisies
covered the hills
like the mantle of some ancient queen
and turned the wheat flat
to a field of gold.
Eva's orchard bloomed—
first the pears,
then the apples,
the blossoms frosting the trees pink and white.
Everywhere, bees hummed.

Early one afternoon,
while Eva was in school,
Eckhart walked up the canyon alone.
He saw things

that he hadn't noticed before—
the way the light
falling on the pine needles
made the trees sparkle like emeralds,
the way the quail bobbed their heads
as they searched for food.
He heard things—
birds singing,
insects clicking, humming, whirring,
leaves pattering.
They're all musicians,
Eckhart thought,
all playing the symphony of the canyon.

For the first time since his parents' death,
Eckhart longed to make music too.
He wanted to pick up the violin
and play—
not for an audience or praise
but because he
wanted
to feel alive,
wanted
to find the music in him,
wanted
to join

in the symphony of the canyon.

When Eckhart reached the meadow,
he saw sun daisies growing
between the foundation stones
of the old homestead.
Eva had said the stones
were like a monument to the pioneers.
How he wished his parents
had a monument
to honor them.

Eckhart threw a stone
into the creek
bubbling through the little gully.
The stone splashed into the water
and clacked against another stone.
Many stones—
big ones,
small ones,
round ones,
flat ones—
gleamed
brown, white, and gold
on the creek bottom.
As Eckhart watched

the water trickling over them,
a thought came to him.
He pulled a paperback book
from his jacket pocket
and stared at the cover.
*The Two Towers*, by J. R. R. Tolkien.

His heart beat faster.
He could build
a tower of stone—
a monument
beside the creek
where he could come
and honor his parents.
He thought of the oath he had sworn—
*By my troth, Mom,*
*I'll find a way to make things right.*
Maybe building a tower
would be a way to do that.

So Eckhart searched
along the creek bank
until he found the perfect place,
a flat spot with a view—
hills to the north and south,
pines and aspens to the west,

and Heaven's Gate Mountain to the east.
He would have to climb
up and down the gully
to haul the rocks out of the creek.
It would be hard—
very hard.

Good.

He scrambled down the gully,
sliding in the loose dirt,
and sloshed into the creek—
searching
for the biggest, flattest stones
he could carry.
Water skittered over his hands
as he pried out the stones.
When he had six,
Eckhart carried them
one by one
up to the flat spot on the bank.
Sweat ran down his back,
his neck,
his face.

Next he fitted the stones together

to make a base for the tower.
It was like doing a puzzle,
finding the best way to snug the rocks.
He took the time to get it right,
then filled in the gaps
with smaller stones.
When the base was about two feet square,
Eckhart stepped back.
Was it big enough?
How high would he build the tower?
As high as he could, he thought,
looking up at Heaven's Gate.
As high as he could.

## Chapter Twenty-Three

Later that afternoon,
his hands scraped and his muscles sore,
Eckhart was walking down the canyon
when he saw Eva coming up.
"I'm building a tower," he told her,
"up above the old homestead."
Eva's eyes turned sparkly. "What fun!
What a fine and noble thing to do."

Eckhart almost told her
about Hell's Canyon,
but something, as always,
held him back.
What if she didn't want
to be friends anymore
once she learned
what a coward he'd been?
Eva was the only friend he had.

So he only said,
"It's a monument to my parents."

"Gramercy!" she exclaimed. "Can I help?"
He thought that over,
and then shook his head.
"I think I should do it alone."
Eva looked quickly away,
hiding her face,
and plucked a wild rose from a bush.
"I understand," she said softly,
twirling the blossom in her fingers
as though it were a tiny umbrella.
"When," she added, "are you going to ask
your uncle about the trial?"

This wasn't the first time
she had asked him this.
"I don't know," Eckhart said,
his eyes sliding away from her.
"But," she persisted,
"you have to know the terms of the trial.
So you can do whatever you need to—
to stay here."
Eckhart kicked a pine cone. "Don't you think
it's braver not to ask?"

"No." Eva shook her head. "I don't.
I think that's just pretending to be brave
when you're really just afraid to ask."

Eckhart felt his face flush red,
felt his tongue twist
into a bolt of lightning.
"Don't call me a coward!" he shouted.
He turned and ran down the canyon.
"Eckhart!" she called.
"That's not what I meant!"

But Eckhart raced
down the path
under the aspens and pines,
raced
until he was panting for breath.
When he reached the deer fence
behind Sunrise Orchard,
he thought he might slip
through the gate
without even opening it,
because he felt about three inches high.
"She's wrong," he said aloud.
"Just plain wrong."

By the time Eckhart reached the house,

his heart had stopped pounding.

Uncle Al and Mr. Salinas stood on the deck.

Even in the warmth of May,

Mr. Salinas wore something wrapped

around and around his big neck—

a blue bandana.

"Let me get this straight, Joe,"

Uncle Al was saying to Mr. Salinas.

"You want me to buy

your Honeycrisp knip-booms?"

"That's right," Mr. Salinas said.


"What are knip-booms?" Eckhart asked.

Annoyed, Uncle Al glanced at him and said,

"A knip-boom is a two-year-old tree

about six feet tall with lots of branches.

Bred for high-density planting."

Eckhart blinked.

Mr. Salinas smiled at him,

then turned back to Uncle Al.

"When I ordered the knip-booms last fall,

I didn't know I'd be selling my place.

Now that you've got the orchard cleaned up,

you need some trees to plant.

I'll give you a good deal, Al."

Uncle Al stared over the field
he and Eckhart had cleared.
Mr. Salinas added, "Honeycrisp apples
are bringing a great return, Al."
"That's so," said Uncle Al.
"But it's years until I'd have a crop.
And a lot of work—
putting in the irrigation pipes,
planting the trees,
building the trellises . . ."
He shook his head. "I don't know, Joe."
Mr. Salinas clapped one hand
on Eckhart's shoulder.
"You have this fine young fellow here
to help you. Wouldn't you like
to see an orchard thriving
on this place again, Eckhart?"

Eckhart nodded. "Yes."
Uncle Al looked at him sharply. "You would?"
"Sure. I like all the trees on Eva's farm.
I was sort of wishing
we had an orchard too."
"It means a lot of work," Uncle Al said.
"Outside work." He raised both eyebrows.

As Eckhart thought that over,
he heard
the meadowlarks singing in the brush—
he saw
the golden daisies waving on the hills—
he felt
the wind blowing down the canyon—
and he realized
that he now liked being outside.
Also, as Eva had just reminded him,
he was still on trial.
If he helped with the Honeycrisp trees,
Uncle Al might let him stay
at Sunrise Orchard.
For now, at least,
it was the only home Eckhart had.
"I can do it," he said at last.
Uncle Al looked skeptical,
but he said, "I'll think it over, Joe."
Mr. Salinas nodded.

That night in his room,
still rattled by his fight with Eva,
Eckhart turned on the 3DS
and The Green Knight.

He had already learned
that the floating white thing
was a veil,
but it continued to elude him—
sometimes appearing,
sometimes disappearing.
He had to get the veil,
had to dip it in holy water
and wipe clean
the walls of the Chapel Perilous.
Only then would the spell
of the Black Hand
be broken.

Again and again
the game killed him.
After the tenth time,
Eckhart gave up.
Usually he could forget everything
when he played,
but tonight he kept remembering
what Eva had said—
that he was just pretending to be brave
when he was really afraid.
What if she were right?

Was he nothing
but a coward at heart?

At last Eckhart fell asleep.
As a violin played
in his dreams,
he dragged stone after stone
up
from the bottom
of the river—
and carried them
one by one
up
to the top
of a mountain.

## Chapter Twenty-Four

The next morning
Eckhart perched on his crate
finishing his cinnamon French toast.
Maybe he wasn't brave enough
to ask his uncle about the trial,
but there was something else
that he did feel brave enough to ask.
"Uncle Al," he blurted,
"I want to start violin lessons again."
"What?" Uncle Al asked
as he stood up from the table.
Eckhart tried again. "I want—
that is,
I'd really like
to have violin lessons again."

Uncle Al stared down at his empty plate
and took a deep breath.

"No," he said flatly.

"But why not? Eckhart asked.

"I know lessons cost a lot,

but maybe the court would give us

money from my trust fund to—"

Uncle Al picked up his plate. "I said no.

Leave it now."

Eckhart started to protest,

but stopped

when he saw the angry glint

in his uncle's eyes.

Uncle Al walked to the sink.

"I'm buying the Honeycrisp trees," he said.

"Let's just do the dishes

and get to work."

So, after the sun rose

from a thicket of clouds,

Eckhart and Uncle Al began

leveling the field

to prepare it for the knip-booms.

Using the blade attachment on the tractor,

they flattened the soil—

turning dark lumps of earth

upward to the light,

like secrets revealed.

Eckhart worked doggedly,
glaring at his uncle
when his back was turned.
Uncle Al himself was like a dark lump of earth,
one still buried,
one with secrets.
He won't stop me from getting violin lessons,
Eckhart thought
as he kicked one of the lumps.
He won't.

Uncle Al let him work
only three hours a day in the field.
So every afternoon,
after his schoolwork was done,
Eckhart walked up the canyon
to work on the tower.

On the first Saturday afternoon in May,
it was nearly eighty degrees
as Eckhart hauled stones
out of the river
and up the steep sides of the gully.
Heat scorched
the open meadow—
but he didn't care.

Sweat ran down his face—
but he didn't care.
His back and arms ached—
but he didn't care.
All that mattered was the tower
getting higher,
bigger,
grander—
and the ache inside him
getting smaller,
lighter.
With each stone
he set in place,
one lifted from his heart.

The creek chattered,
but Eckhart didn't mind the sound—
it encouraged him,
and it wasn't a roar.

"Wow!" said a voice.
Eva stood beside him.
"The tower is almost as tall
as your chest, Eckhart."
She held out a thermos. "Lemonade.
A peace offering."

On a cord round her neck,

a silver goblet hung

like a pendant on a necklace.

Eckhart looked at the thermos,

at the goblet,

then up at her face.

They hadn't met since their fight.

Her green eyes looked wary,

and suddenly he felt sorry for that.


"It was stupid—" he began.

"I'm sorry—" she said.

Then Eckhart smiled,

and Eva smiled back.

"You were right," he said. "I was afraid

to ask my uncle about the trial.

Afraid of what he might say,

that I might not be able to do

what he wants."

"It's just that," Eva began,

"I don't want . . .

I don't want you to . . ."

She looked away.


Then she unlooped the goblet

from the cord,

pressed a button on the thermos,
and poured a golden stream into the goblet.
She set the thermos down.
Cupping the goblet in both hands,
Eva held it up to him.
The sun shone brightly on the metal,
and silver light spilled
across her fingers.
"For you," she said.

After the cold, sweet liquid
ran down his throat,
Eckhart said, "I asked Uncle Al
for violin lessons."
"What did he say?" Eva asked.
"He said no.
He wouldn't even talk about it.
And he looked mad—really mad."
Eva's eyes widened. "That's strange."
Eckhart took another sip of lemonade.
"I thought I wouldn't mind
staying here until I found my real home.
But now, without music lessons,
I don't know if I want to stay at all."

Eva opened her mouth,

then shut it again.

She picked up the thermos,

hugged it tightly,

and rested her chin on top.

After Eckhart finished the lemonade,

he gave the silver goblet back to her.

"I better get back to work.

Thanks for the lemonade."

And he went down to the creek.

When he climbed up

with yet another stone

in his hands,

Eva was gone.

## Chapter Twenty-Five

The next Monday morning,
Eckhart and Uncle Al finished leveling the field.
They began marking out
the orchard rows with stakes.
Eckhart wore a baseball hat,
sunscreen, and a long-sleeved T-shirt,
but as the days passed,
he grew brown anyway.

After the rows were marked out,
Uncle Al used an attachment on the tractor
to dig trenches for the irrigation pipes.
Eckhart glued the white plastic pipes
together in endless lines.
Now and then he glanced up
at Heaven's Gate Mountain.
He imagined the tower for his parents

rising in the canyon—
rising higher
and higher
until it soared like Heaven's Gate.


By Friday afternoon,
the tower stood higher than his head.
Yet Eckhart kept hauling stones
out of the creek.
He liked fitting them together,
liked searching for the right rock
for the right space.
Eva came walking up to him,
her jeans swishing in the tall meadow grass.
"Hi," she called,
waving a rolled-up tube of paper
tied with a red ribbon.
"What's that?" Eckhart asked.
"It's a contract—
written in my best calligraphy.
For you and your uncle."
She untied the ribbon,
unrolled the paper,
and held it up to him.
He read:

This contract,

entered into in the month of May _____ ,

is between Albert Reed (the uncle)

and Eckhart Lyon (his nephew).

It lists the ten tasks Eckhart must do in order to

(one:)

have violin lessons

and

(two:)

STAY FOREVER

on Sunrise Orchard.

Mr. Reed agrees that when these tasks

are satisfactorily completed,

Eckhart will have earned a home (and violin lessons)

FOREVER AND EVER.

Below were lines for signatures.
Eva pointed to a list of numbers one through ten
with blank spaces beside them.
"That's where you and your uncle
can write in tasks," she explained.
"This will make it easier for you
to talk to him about the trial."
She beamed.

"Thanks," Eckhart mumbled.
He wished she would stop
bothering him about this.
Besides, he wasn't sure
he wanted to stay
at Sunrise Orchard forever.
But Eva might be right—
the contract might help him
talk to his uncle.
"You can do it, Eckhart," she said softly.
"I know you can."
"I better get back to work," he said,
and picked up another rock.

"I think the tower is finished," Eva said.
Startled, Eckhart paused
with the rock in his hands.

"How do you know?" he asked.
"Same way I know when a poem is finished.
Stand back and look at it."
He did.

The tower was round—
it was tall—
thicker at the bottom
and narrower at the top—
it was mighty—
it was perfect.
Eckhart nodded.
"One more stone would ruin it," he said,
and tossed away the rock in his hand.
"It's finished."

Eva said, "Let's have a dedication ceremony.
But . . . don't you think
the tower needs a name first?"
Eckhart nodded. "I assent me."
"Good. While you think of a name,
I'll pick some flowers for the ceremony."
Eckhart thought.
Many names passed through his mind,
some too grand,
some too plain,

none just right.

Then it came to him.


"I know," he said when Eva came back,

"let's call it the Tower of Troth."

"Wonderful!" Eva exclaimed.

She held out a bunch of wildflowers. "May I?"

Eckhart nodded.

He thought she would lay the bouquet

at the foot of the tower.

Instead Eva pulled out a red flower

and tucked it in a crevice

between two rocks.

"The blessing of paintbrush," she said.

She tucked in a white flower—

"The blessing of wild rose."

A yellow flower—

"The blessing of balsam."

A pink one—

"The blessing of shooting star . . ."

Solemnly she worked her way

up and down and around the stones

until the whole tower

quivered with flowers.


The tower looked like something from a fairy tale—

a tower of old,
and Eckhart almost expected to see
knights and ladies
ride gaily out of it
on their way to a tournament.

After placing the last flower,
Eva turned toward him,
her brown hair glinting almost red
in the sunlight.
She looked like a great Lady
in an old tale.
"And I name you," he said to her,
"the Lady of the Canyon."

Her cheeks turned pink.
"Gramercy," she whispered.
Then she looked expectantly at him.
"You need to say something—
for the dedication."
Eckhart thought for a moment,
then spoke.
"May this tower—
the Tower of Troth—
stand forever
in memory of my mom and dad,

Rose and Gordon Lyon."

And as he watched the flower petals
flutter in the breeze—
so delicate,
so fleeting next to the enduring stone—
Eckhart felt a lightness in his heart,
and he laughed suddenly,
laughed for no reason
but the lightness.

## Chapter Twenty-Six

After dinner that evening
the air hovered,
hot and sultry.
Up in his room
Eckhart pulled his mom's violin case
out from under his bed.
Dust filmed the top,
and he wiped it clean.
Then, kneeling beside the case,
he unhooked the latches
and opened it for the first time
since she had died.

In the lamplight
the violin gleamed
the color of maple syrup.
Eckhart blinked hard.
He tended to the humidifier,

then pressed one finger against the wood
by the sound hole.
The violin felt warm,
as though it were a living thing.

Eckhart felt an ache inside
that was not sadness
but a longing for music,
a longing for joy.
Part of him wanted to grab the violin,
tighten the bow,
and play the song from Bach's Chaconne
that his mom had written
just for him.
Instead he plucked the A string.
The sound swelled through the room,
hung
in the hot air,
hung
inside him—
one drop in the sea of ache.

He shut the case.

Eckhart turned on The Green Knight.
He had already found the white veil.

The world and the night
dropped away
as he searched
for the holy well
to dip the white veil into.
Then he entered a courtyard
filled with statues of fantastic beasts.
An instant later
the beasts attacked.

He fought his way
toward an ancient apple tree
laden with golden apples.
There! He spotted a pile of stones
by the roots.
He tossed the stones aside,
and before him lay the holy well.
Kneeling,
Eckhart dipped the veil into the water.

At last he had everything
to defeat the Black Hand—
the spear,
the sword,
the helm,

and the veil damp with holy water.
He raced back to the Chapel Perilous
to wipe down the walls.
Again the Black Hand
scuttled forward
to extinguish the candle.

Suddenly the game changed.

A knight cloaked in green
with a glittering ax
appeared before the altar.
In front of him
stood a chopping block.
Confused, Eckhart hesitated—
and the Black Hand sprang,
and the candle went out,
and Eckhart fell
into a howling wind,
fell
and fell—
down
into darkness.

An hour later

a storm woke him.
Wind careened
from the northern hills.
Swords of lightning
battled in the sky,
bellowing thunder.
Eckhart went downstairs
and stood outside
under the covered porch
by the antler trees,
which swayed and clicked
in the wind.
Rain flung
itself from the clouds
in a frenzy,
drumming on the metal roof—
Like the fingernails
of the Black Hand, Eckhart thought.

Uncle Al came up behind him.
"I haven't seen it rain
this hard in years," he said
as the lightning flashed again.
Five seconds later
thunder exploded like a bomb

and shook the old house.
The lights flickered
once,
twice—
then everything went black.

## Chapter Twenty-Seven

Standing on the covered deck
with the storm howling around him,
Eckhart blinked,
trying to adjust his eyes
to the sudden darkness.
"Stay here," Uncle Al said,
"until I get a flashlight.
Don't want you falling off the deck."
So Eckhart waited,
listening to the rain.
Storm clouds hid the moon and stars,
making the night utterly black.
He thought about Frodo the turtle,
who could curl up
inside his shell
to protect himself from a storm.
Eckhart hoped Frodo had found a home
where he was safe and warm.

A few minutes later
Eckhart and Uncle Al were inside the house
with the candles lit.
The storm rolled on.
"No use trying to sleep," Uncle Al said.
"Can you play cards?"
Eckhart nodded.
So, by the light of seven candles,
they played rummy.
To Eckhart's surprise
Uncle Al played well,
winning three games
to Eckhart's one.
After the fourth game
they sat silently
listening to the storm.

Eckhart eyed Eva's contract,
lying beside his schoolbooks on the couch.
He tapped his foot.
Tomorrow she would ask
if he had shown Uncle Al the contract.
Tap, Eckhart's foot went—
tap, tap.
His uncle glanced at him.

"Something on your mind?"

Eckhart nodded,
half rose to get the contract,
then sat back down on the crate.
Thunder boomed.
Taking a deep breath,
he walked over to the couch
and picked up the contract.

"What's that?" Uncle Al asked
when Eckhart returned to the table.
Eckhart slid the contract
through his fingers.
He asked, "How come you and Lily
and Aunt Irina never came to visit us?"
Uncle Al started shuffling the cards.
"Because Rose—your mom—
and I didn't get along. Old family stuff."

Shadows cast by the flickering candles
moved across Uncle Al's face.
His hands, shuffling the cards,
moved in and out of the light—
white,

black,

white,

black. . . .

Eckhart tugged the ribbon on the contract

and glanced sideways at his uncle.

"Uncle Al, when will the trial be over?"

"It'll be over when it's over," Uncle Al said.


Not good enough, Eckhart thought.

I need a home now.

I need violin lessons.

He glanced at the sheepskin on the couch

for courage.

Then, with shaking hands,

Eckhart untied the red ribbon

and unrolled the contract.


"What is that?" Uncle Al asked again.

"A contract."

Uncle Al blinked. "A contract? For what?"

"For the trial. We can list everything

I need to do for the trial to be over.

I want to know . . .

I need to know . . ."

He faltered

because his uncle was frowning.
Outside, rain beat
against the curtainless window,
raw with night.
"I thought," Eckhart added,
holding out the contract,
"we could fill it in together and sign it."

Uncle Al took the contract.
He read it fast,
and then looked up,
his eyes angry. "Violin lessons?
You're demanding violin lessons?"
He shook his head.
"You know why I didn't get along with your mom?
Because of violin lessons."
Lightning flashed
and illuminated Uncle Al's face—
revealing every wrinkle,
every crag,
every scar—
like the bark of some old tree.
"Rose's talent always came first," he said.
"Every penny our parents had
went for her violin lessons, her teachers,

her college at Juilliard.
There was nothing left for me.
Nobody cared about my dreams."

Eckhart felt
his back rounding,
his shoulders hunching,
his toes curling
as he tried to shrink inside himself.
He gripped the crate
until the wood
bit into his hands.

His uncle raged on.
"Our father promised me
all the inheritance money—
all of it—
to make up for what they spent on Rose.
But after he died last summer,
I learned he'd never changed his will.
So Rose got half."
Uncle Al balled up the contract,
crushing Eva's calligraphy.
"Know what Rose did
with all that money

that should have been mine?"

Swallowing hard, Eckhart nodded
his head with the tiniest of nods.
"That's right," Uncle Al said.
"She bought that fancy Italian violin.
Five hundred thousand dollars for a *violin*."
He slapped the table.
"And now you are asking me
for violin lessons?"

Uncle Al threw the balled-up contract
across the room.
It bounced off the woodstove.
Cub, lying on the sheepskin,
raised his head and sniffed the wad of paper.
Uncle Al jumped up,
snatched it,
and strode back to the table,
shaking the paper in his fist.

Eckhart jumped up,
and the crate crashed to the floor.
Uncle Al shouted, "You want to know
when the trial will be over?
You want to know?

I'll tell you.
When you give me that violin!"
He grabbed his coat
and strode out the door—
into the night,
into the storm.

## Chapter Twenty-Eight

When Eckhart woke the next morning
and looked out the round window,
sun soaked the sky.
He didn't get up.
He dreaded going downstairs
and facing his uncle.
In a sudden panic
he reached under the bed—
the violin was still there,
it was still there.
He sighed with relief.

Sunlight fell
on Lily's drawing
of the crooked crayon house
with the blue heart-shaped door,
the red lollipop flowers,
and the sun rising over a hill.
Eckhart wondered

if it was Lily's idea of home.

"This isn't home!" he exclaimed,
throwing off the red wool blanket.
In his real home
no one would shout at him.
In his real home
no one would make him choose
between staying and his mom's violin.
In his real home . . .
Eckhart grabbed his pillow—
his pillow that smelled of wind and sun—
and threw it across the room.
He wanted to kick something,
shout,
scream,
rage.

Someone knocked on the front door.

When Eckhart stuck his head out the window
and saw Eva,
his heart turned hard and brittle—
like a bone.
It was her fault,
all her fault,

that Uncle Al had been so mean.
If she hadn't made that contract,
Uncle Al wouldn't have demanded the violin.


Eva looked up and saw him.
"Come down!" she shouted.
Eckhart shook his head.
"I'm tired," he called.
She waved one hand. "Oh, come on!
We have to check on the canyon.
See what the storm did.
There are always big changes
after a storm."


Eckhart stood glaring at her,
but curiosity overcame him.
"Oh, all right," he called. "I'm coming."
After he was dressed,
he went down the spiral staircase
and grabbed an apple from the counter.
Then he opened the door.
Eva grinned. "Wasn't the storm fun?"
Without answering,
without looking at her,
Eckhart bit into the apple.
"What's wrong?" Eva asked.

Eckhart shook his head. "Nothing."
"Good. Let's go, then."

Eckhart knew he should ask
permission before going up the canyon,
but he didn't want to see his uncle.
As he chewed the apple,
the pulp seemed to stick in his throat,
so he tossed the rest of the apple away.
He didn't care if he got into trouble.
He didn't care about anything.

Up the canyon they went.
Branches fallen from the aspens and pines
littered the trail.
In places whole trees had blown down—
one aspen blocked the trail.
"Someone will have to cut this out
with the chain saw," Eva said,
"so we can ski next winter.
And look over there!
The creek changed its path!"
The once gentle creek
was now a raging, swollen torrent,
carving new channels
along the bank.

When they reached the meadow,
they checked on the Chapel Perilous.
The screen of pine boughs sagged,
and some of the bones lay shattered
on the ground.
"That's easily fixed," Eva said.
"There are plenty of bones in the canyon."
Eckhart said, "Let's go to the Tower of Troth."
Maybe the sight of it
would cool the burning in his stomach
and help him decide
what to do about the violin,
the trial,
and his uncle.

They walked on up the creek,
until they found a safe place
to cross on boulders.
When at last they reached
the site of the Tower of Troth,
Eva cried out,
and Eckhart's breath burst from him
as though he'd been punched.

The Tower of Troth was gone.

# Chapter Twenty-Nine

The creek had ripped away the bank
where the Tower of Troth had stood.
All of the stones
Eckhart had so laboriously hauled,
all of the stones
he had so carefully fitted together,
lay tumbled
on the bottom of the raging creek.

"No," Eckhart whispered,
"no."
The monument to his parents
was destroyed.
A sob rose in his throat—
as though they had died
all over again.
Shouting,
he kicked at the dirt—

shouting, kicking, screaming.

Eva stood quietly.
When he fell silent at last,
she came and slipped her hand into his.
But Eckhart sprang away from her.
"You!" he exclaimed.
"You and your stupid contract!
I showed it to my uncle last night,
and he got really, really mad.
He said the trial wouldn't be over
until I give him my mom's violin!"
"Wh-what?" Eva stammered, her eyes big.
Eckhart glared at her.
"If you hadn't pushed me into asking him,
it wouldn't have happened!"
He kicked a rock.
"Now I have to choose.
A home or my mom's violin!"

Eva sat down,
sat right down on the bank
of the rushing creek
and dropped her head in her hands.
"I'm sorry," she said. "I—"
"Why?" Eckhart interrupted.

"Why did you push me so hard
to ask about the trial?"
Slowly Eva looked up at him.
"Because . . . of Chloe.
I lost her.
My last best friend. And I . . .
I don't want you to go away too.
Not ever."

Eckhart's anger shattered
into crumbs. "You don't?
But sometimes you don't even want
to do stuff together.
I never go to your house.
You hardly ever come to mine.
We're only friends here in the canyon."
Eva picked a sun daisy
and started pulling off the petals.
"I felt so sad when Chloe went away.
It hurt. Like a big hole in my heart.
So I was scared . . . if you went away too,
there'd be another hole like that."

Eckhart watched the petals fall
one by one into her lap,
then sat down beside her.

"But I thought . . . ," he said,
"I mean, you said your heart's desire
was to find a new best friend."
She nodded. "It is.
But I want a best friend
who won't go away.
I thought if I kept you
as a canyon friend,
you'd be part of the magic here.
Then it wouldn't hurt . . .
if you went away."

Eckhart stiffened,
afraid she might ask him
to give up the violin so he could stay
on Sunrise Orchard.
"That violin is all . . ."
He took in a shuddering breath.
"It's all I have left of my mom,
especially now that the tower is gone."
"I know," Eva said. "I'm sorry.
Sorry for everything."
She stared at the creek. "I can't believe
the tower is gone."

As Eckhart watched the water

swirl over the ruins
of the Tower of Troth,
his heart shriveled.
"I tried," he said,
"tried so hard
to make things right.
I failed."
Eva shook her head. "You didn't fail.
You did what you set out to do.
You completed your task,
like a true knight would.
The storm wasn't your fault."

Eckhart closed his eyes,
took a deep breath,
then opened them again.
"But what am I supposed to do now?" he asked.
"How do you make something you did wrong,
terribly wrong,
right again?"
Eva gazed at the sun daisy petals
piled in her lap,
a thoughtful look on her face.
"You could start by apologizing,"
she suggested, smiling a little.
"It made me feel better just now."

He shook his head. "That won't work.
The people I'd apologize to are . . ."
he swallowed hard—
"are dead."

She looked up.
"Your parents?" she asked softly.
He nodded.
Eva gathered the golden petals.
"Then you must atone," she said.
"Atone?"
"Yes. To atone is to right a wrong."
Eckhart remembered
what Uncle Al had said
about finding a way to make things right.
"But how do I . . . atone?" Eckhart asked.
"What should I do?"
"Let me think." And Eva threw the petals
into the air
where the tower had stood.
Whirling like golden wishes,
they fell into the creek,
where the current danced them away.

"Often," she said at last,
"in the days of old,

people who wanted to atone
went on pilgrimages—
journeys to a shrine,
a church,
or some other sacred place."
Eckhart eyed her doubtfully.
"Where would I go around here?"
He didn't want to go to a church
and tell some strange priest or pastor
about Hell's Canyon.

Eva's eyes lit up. "I know!
There is a place—
a sacred place right here in the canyon
that I haven't told you about."
"What sacred place?" Eckhart asked.
"You'll see." Eva jumped up.
"Come on!"

# Chapter Thirty

Eckhart and Eva started up the meadow,
startling a covey of quail
that burst from the brush
and flew away
toward Heaven's Gate Mountain.
Eckhart asked, "Why haven't you
shown me this place before?"
Eva glance sideways at him.
"I was afraid
you'd laugh at me.
But I know you well enough now
to share it with you.
And I think it will help."

Some fifty yards into the meadow,
Eva stopped and turned,
pointing at the southern hill.
"There!" she exclaimed. "Look!"

Eckhart did,
but all he saw was a snag—
the pointed, snaggy top of an old stump—
sticking out of the hilltop.
"I only see a stump," he said.
"That's no stump," Eva said,
"that is Good Wizard.
I made him out of magic."
Puzzled, Eckhart looked at her.
"That snag used to scare me," she explained.
"I even called it the Demon Snag.
So, with the Greater Power of my Imagination,
I changed him into Good Wizard.
Now he watches over the canyon.
Doesn't he look like he's wearing
a robe and a pointy wizard's hat?"

Eckhart studied the stump.
Tall, tapering to a point at the top,
it did look like a hunched person
wearing a robe.
He stared at Eva in awe.
She could make
something wonderful
out of anything—
petals,

bones,

stumps—

as though the whole world

were her violin.


Eckhart looked back at Good Wizard.

One branch, sticking out like an arm,

had a round knob on the end.

"He looks like he's holding a ball."

"Exactly!" she exclaimed.

"I knew you'd see it.

I call this Wizard's Meadow.

And I think you should make a pilgrimage

up to Good Wizard—

ask him how to atone

for whatever you did wrong."


Eckhart stared at the steep hill.

"It's a long way up there," he said.

"A pilgrimage is supposed to be hard,"

Eva pointed out.

"Otherwise it's not worth doing.

And I think you should take an offering."

"An offering?" Eckhart asked.

Eva nodded. "To appease Good Wizard.

So he will look favorably

on your request.

Some kind of sacrifice."

She grew solemn. "It must be something
you value greatly."

Eckhart thought.

"But I don't have anything with me."

"We can't go now anyway," she said.

"We have to prepare."

"We?" he asked.

"Tomorrow's Sunday," Eva explained.

"No school. So I'll go with you after church—
if you want."

Eckhart nodded. "I assent me."

"Bring water and wear boots," she added.

"I'll meet you
at the Chapel Perilous at noon."

## Chapter Thirty-One

After Eckhart came down
from the canyon,
he skulked outside the house,
avoiding his uncle.
He wandered over
to the dented camping trailer
on the north side of the shop.
The door squeaked
when he stepped inside.
In front of him was a counter
with a hot plate and a rust-stained sink.
To his left were two bunk beds.
To his right stood a table
with an old-time typewriter—
not even electric—
on top of it.
Someone had typed a few words
on a sheet of paper in the rollers.

Eckhart leaned forward and read:

*PEACH SEASON*
*a novel*
*by*
*Albert Reed*

*In the season of peaches, when the air*
*holds the last sweetness of summer,*
*a woman walked into a*

That was all.
His uncle was a writer?
Dust filmed the typewriter,
as though it hadn't been used
in a long time.

Then Eckhart heard footsteps
crunching on the gravel outside—
Uncle Al.
Eckhart ducked down,
holding his breath.
He didn't want his uncle to find him
in the trailer.
The footsteps paused by the trailer door,
then went past.

Eckhart waited five minutes
before slipping outside.

Hunger finally drove him
back to the house.
He paused in the doorway,
watching Uncle Al,
who was standing at the kitchen counter
spreading peanut butter on bread.
"Sandwich?" Uncle Al asked
without looking up.
"Sure," Eckhart mumbled.

In silence
they ate their sandwiches
at the picnic table on the deck.
In silence
the ghost of last night's storm
hovered over them.
In silence
Eckhart chewed
and swallowed
and wondered.
Maybe the trial had only
been a pretense.
Maybe his uncle had only

wanted the violin all along.

He's never wanted *me*, Eckhart thought,

ripping off a bite of sandwich.

Never.


After dinner

Eckhart searched through his belongings

for something to sacrifice to Good Wizard.

*Something of value*, Eva had said.

There were his books—

his set of *The Lord of the Rings*,

and his King Arthur books.

He sat down on his bed

and opened his battered copy

of *The Boy's King Arthur*.

Inside the cover

his mom had written:


> *To Eckhart on his tenth birthday:*
> *You will always be my knight in*
> *shining armor.*
> *Love, Mom*


Eckhart's heart ached

because he had not been that at all.

He had not saved her.

His dad—
Eckhart saw him diving
from the boulder
into the deadly river
to try to save Eckhart's mom.
Eckhart jumped up from the bed.
"You were safe, Dad!" he exclaimed.
"You'd still be here . . ."
He slammed the book shut—
angry
because his dad had left him all alone—
angry
because his dad had made them go rafting—
angry
because his dad had been the knight in shining armor
instead of him.

Eckhart put the book away.
He'd lost too much of his mom
already
to sacrifice the book
to Good Wizard.
Eckhart glanced around,
searching for something else,
and his eyes fell on his 3DS.
Something clutched in his stomach.

No.

Not that.

Eckhart sat down on his bed

beside the 3DS,

not looking at it,

not moving.

He sat there for a long time.


A *pilgrimage is supposed to be hard,*

Eva had said.

*Otherwise it's not worth doing.*

His mom's frightened face,

as he had last seen it in the river,

flashed into his mind.

*My knight . . .*

*in shining armor . . .*

*My knight . . .*

"By my troth, Mom," he whispered.

"I will make it right."


Sinking back on his pillow,

Eckhart scanned the menu

on his iPod.

He wanted something bright,

yet fierce and strong.

Then he knew.

Bach's Chaconne—
the last piece he had
heard his mother play.
As the opening chords sounded,
Eckhart turned on his 3DS,
and played The Green Knight
deep into the dark hours—
played as though
the playing would save him,
though he knew by now
it wouldn't.

Again and again,
armed with sword and spear and helm,
carrying the veil dipped in holy water,
he faced the Green Knight—
who stood before the block
with the glittering ax.
Flames leaped
in a ring of fire
around the block.

Then Eckhart saw he needed
one last knightly tool—
a shield.
As he played,

he at last fell asleep.
And in his nightmare
he bared his neck
upon the burning block
as the Green Knight
raised high his ax.

## Chapter Thirty-Two

At noon the next day,
his eyes bleary from lack of sleep,
Eckhart met Eva
at the Chapel Perilous.
Her shining white shirt
rippled to the knees of her jeans.
"I found this shirt," she explained,
"at the thrift store in Twisp.
We can imagine it's white samite—
that's a kind of cloth
that priestesses and knights of old wore."
Around her neck was a silver cord
with a round, pink stone
hanging on the end of it.
"Did you bring your sacrifice?" she asked.
Eckhart pulled the 3DS
out of his backpack
and held it up.

Eva's eyes widened. "Wow.

You must really be serious about this."

"I am."

"Then place it on the altar," Eva said.

He did.

"I brought a sacrifice too," she said,

laying a golden envelope beside the 3DS.

"Now we must kneel."

They did.

Eva raised her arms.

"We call on the spirits of the canyon

to watch over us on our pilgrimage.

May the bones of the hills support us.

May the pines uplift us.

May these offerings

be acceptable to Good Wizard

so that he may look favorably

upon our humble requests.

In God we trust. Amen."

She poked her elbow into Eckhart's side.

"Amen," he repeated.


She blew out the candle. "Let's go."

Eckhart slipped the 3DS

inside his backpack.

Eva took off the white shirt—

she wore a green T-shirt underneath—
and stuffed it inside her own backpack.
Then, their water bottles sloshing,
they left the Chapel Perilous.

"I think," Eva said, pointing,
"we should go back down the canyon
and then walk up Stagecoach Road
to the top of Stagecoach Hill.
From there we can follow the ridgeline
all the way up to Good Wizard.
There's no trail."
Squinting into the sun,
Eckhart asked,
"Have you ever been up
to see Good Wizard before?"
Eva shook her head.

Back down the canyon they went
until they found Stagecoach Road.
The old road curled up the hill.
The wagon ruts cut deep,
choked with what Eva said was pigweed,
though to Eckhart
it looked like white flowers.
Yellow sun daisies

waved like banners on the hill,
and as they walked,
Eckhart found himself wondering
if they had entered some tale of old.
Halfway up the hill
he began panting,
but, determined to keep up with Eva,
he didn't slow down.

"We turn off the road here," Eva said,
"and start following the ridge."
Eckhart looked at the ridge
sloping steadily upward.
Already his heart was pounding,
his breath coming fast and hard.
Could he make it all the way up?

Eva looked at him. "I call a water break."
"I assent me," Eckhart said,
and reached for his water bottle.
"I have apple juice cartons," Eva said.
"According to legend,
apples are the fruit of the otherworld.
So it would be wise to drink the juice."
Eckhart took the offered carton,
pulled off the straw,

and poked it inside.
The juice tasted sweet and cold
on his tongue.
He drank it all.

They went on.

As the ridge climbed up and up,
Eckhart went slower and slower,
plodding around
the sagebrush and the bitterbrush.
Now and then Eva would stop
and exclaim over the wildflowers
that bloomed so briefly
on the hills in spring.
But soon, too soon
it always seemed to Eckhart,
they went on again.

At last Eva stopped,
pointing up the ridge. "Look!
That's Good Wizard!
We're almost there."
They toiled another fifty yards
up the ridge
and finally reached Good Wizard.

The snag loomed up
three times the height of a man—
much taller,
much bigger
than it had looked
from the bottom of the canyon.
Black streaks scarred one side
of the gray wood.
Eva said, "Lightning might have hit it once,
or maybe a fire killed it.
Wildfires can break out anytime
in hot weather."
Pink shooting stars circled
the bottom of the old stump—
as though Good Wizard
stood in a cloud of magic.

Eva bowed.
"Hail, Good Wizard," she called.
"I, Evangeline DeHart,
and this boy, Eckhart Lyon,
give you greeting.
We have come on pilgrimage
to ask your advice.
And we bring you offerings
of great worth."

She nodded at Eckhart.
"Hail, Good Wizard," he said.

She took out her golden envelope,
and he took out his 3DS.
"Good Wizard," she said,
"I offer you this poem,
a poem that no one else has ever seen
or ever shall.
And I humbly request
that I might find my heart's desire—
a new best friend."
She tucked the golden envelope
into a crack in the stump.
"Your turn," she whispered to Eckhart.

Slowly,
very slowly,
Eckhart approached Good Wizard
with the 3DS clasped in his hands.
"Good Wizard," he began,
"I offer you my 3DS,
and humbly request
that you tell me how to atone
for my mom's death."
Eva glanced at him

but didn't speak.

Eckhart stepped forward,
then stopped
and stared down at the 3DS.
Without it
he would never finish The Green Knight—
never find his shield,
never stop the Black Hand
from snuffing out the light.

Then a bird called,
and he looked up.
"A meadowlark," Eva said softly.

Eckhart looked out at all the world—
at the white clouds
blossoming across the blue sky—
at the hills,
dusky gold, olive, and brown—
at the canyon far below,
the treetops a haze of green.
All the world was filled with light,
all the world waited.

Eckhart stepped forward

and wedged the 3DS
between two gnarled roots.
"Tell me, Good Wizard," he said,
"what I can do to make things right."

The wind rose,
whistling though the stump,
and it seemed as though Good Wizard himself
were whistling
as he pondered Eckhart's question.
A pine tree swayed,
and Eva's hair blew in ribbons
around her face.
Good Wizard whistled louder.
Eckhart blinked,
for the wizard's arm-like branch
pointed straight
to the top
of Heaven's Gate Mountain.

As the wind rose
and rose,
as the whistling pierced
the scars and the weariness
in Eckhart's heart,
as he became light,

so light,
almost lifting from the ridge—
Eckhart knew
exactly what he had to do
to atone.

He had to go higher.
He had to go
all the way
to the very top
of Heaven's Gate.

# PART 3:

# The Quest of Heaven's Gate

## Chapter Thirty-Three

After bowing good-bye
to Good Wizard,
Eckhart and Eva climbed silently down the ridge.
Eckhart kept glancing backward,
searching for the silver flash
of his 3DS in Good Wizard's roots.

They didn't speak
until they reached Stagecoach Road.
Then Eva said in an awed voice,
"Good Wizard whistled for us!
I'm using all the Greater Power of my Imagination
to figure out what he was saying."
She scrambled over a log.
"I think I know," Eckhart said,
and he told her how Good Wizard
had pointed him to Heaven's Gate Mountain.
Eva clapped her hands. "A quest!

Good Wizard is sending you on a quest!
Are you going to do it?"

Eckhart answered
in the language of knights: "I will well.
I'm going to climb all the way
to the top of Heaven's Gate.
And I have to go alone."
Eva nodded. "I assent me."
"I'll ask my uncle if I can go tomorrow."
"I wouldn't," Eva said.
Eckhart stopped. "Why not?"
"Because he won't let you go so far alone.
Besides," she added gently,
"you're not ready
to climb that high."

Eckhart thought this over.
It was true
that he had barely made it to Good Wizard.
Even now his legs shook from the strain.
And Heaven's Gate was much higher.
"Then what should I do?" he asked.
"You prepare," Eva said firmly.
"Knights must often prepare
for their quests. You must train

for the Quest of Heaven's Gate."
Eckhart stepped around a boulder
that had fallen onto Stagecoach Road.
Soon they would reach
the welcome shade of the canyon.
"What kind of training?" he asked.

"Well," Eva said,
"you might climb this hill
three times a day, walking first,
then running when you're stronger.
When you can run
up and down Stagecoach Hill
three times without stopping,
you'll be ready for Heaven's Gate."
Eckhart nodded. "I will well.
I'll start training tomorrow."
She grinned.
"I bet you'll be too sore tomorrow."

After lunch Eckhart felt so tired
from the climb up the ridge
that he lay down on his bed
and fell asleep.
Not until three o'clock
did he wake to the whine

of the lawn mower outside.
Eckhart stood up.
His legs felt stiff and sore,
and he moved as slowly
as an old man.

The next two weeks whirled by
so fast that Eckhart barely missed his 3DS.
First thing each morning,
before it grew hot,
Eckhart climbed up Stagecoach Road.
He walked,
then ran until he panted for breath,
and then walked again.
Afterward he helped Uncle Al
prepare the field
for the knip-boom Honeycrisp trees.

After the main irrigation pipes were laid,
they added risers to them—
the pipes with sprinkler heads on top.
They would stick up from the ground
after the main pipes were buried.
This took days.
Then Uncle Al said,
"Now we go down each row

and mark where the holes
should be dug for the trees—
one every thirty-nine inches."

So Eckhart and Uncle Al crawled
along the ground
with a measuring stick
and a can of spray paint.
After measuring off thirty-nine inches,
Eckhart shook the can.
The ball inside rattled like a metal maraca.
He pressed the nozzle
and sprayed a red X on the dirt,
like marking a spot
for buried treasure.
Then he did it all again.
And again.
It took forever.
At night he dreamed of red Xs
swirling on rivers
and marching up mountains.

He and his uncle seldom spoke
as they worked.
Neither of them ever mentioned
what had happened the night of the storm.

But—

as the metal maraca played,

as the paint hissed from the can,

as the red Xs filled the field,

Eckhart felt ghosts hovering over them—

his mom's violin,

the inheritance money,

the trial,

his music lessons,

and Uncle Al's anger.

Eckhart didn't know what to do

about any of it,

except work hard.

Maybe then he could change his uncle's mind.

So he crawled,

he measured,

he rattled the metal maraca,

and sprayed X

after X

after endless X—

all in the hope of finding treasure.

# Chapter Thirty-Four

One morning,
the last day of May,
Eckhart ran up and down
Stagecoach Hill without stopping.
Soon, he thought.
Soon he would be able to run up
three times in a row.
Then he could go
on the Quest of Heaven's Gate.

Later that same morning
Eckhart and Uncle Al
were working in the field
when a black Toyota Corolla rumbled up
the gravel road and stopped.
A woman in a red suit stepped out,
shaded her eyes, and waved.
"Who's that?" Eckhart asked Uncle Al.

"The social worker from Wenatchee.
The one who first came to tell me about you."
"What does she want?" Eckhart asked.
Uncle Al sighed. "Let's go see."

So they crossed the field of red Xs
to where the woman stood waiting.
"Why, Mr. Reed," she said,
in a voice too bright and cheery.
"It sure is nice to see you again.
I'm Mrs. Bletcher, as you may recall.
And this fine-looking boy here
must surely be Eckhart."
She smiled so wide that Eckhart feared
her bright red lips might fly
off her face.
"Yes, ma'am. He is," Uncle Al said.
"Wonderful. I came to see how Eckhart is doing."
"He's doing fine," Uncle Al said.
"We're busy here.
Why didn't you send a letter
telling me you were coming?"
Mrs. Bletcher's smile faded,
then an even larger one
swooped across her face.
"Oh, it's our policy to do surprise visits.

I'm sure you understand."

She gazed over the field.

"Working hard, I see.

Perhaps it's time Eckhart was back in school."

Eckhart spoke up.

"I work in my schoolbooks every day.

And there are only a few weeks left

before summer. I'd have to be with a bunch

of strange kids. I'd rather wait until fall."

He glanced at Uncle Al. "If, that is,

I'm still here then."

Uncle Al didn't say anything.

"I'd rather wait," Eckhart repeated.

"Well, now," Mrs. Bletcher said,

"don't you think that's for the doctor to say?"

"Doctor?" asked Eckhart and Uncle Al together.

"Why, yes." Her penciled eyebrows soared up.

Eckhart wondered if all her features

were trying to fly off her face.

She added, "Eckhart was let off school

due to doctor's orders—

a Seattle doctor." She sniffed with disdain.

"But he wanted Eckhart

to be examined again in three months.

I'm sure I told you that, Mr. Reed."
Uncle Al grunted.
"I've taken the liberty," she said,
"of setting up an appointment for Eckhart
next Thursday afternoon
with Dr. McCollum in Wenatchee.
And I'm sure you'll agree, Mr. Reed,
that doctors on our side of the state
are more sensible than those Seattle doctors."

"I have my own doctor," Uncle Al said.
"The boy can see him."
Mrs. Bletcher frowned. "I'm afraid
it's the department's policy
to have Eckhart see a doctor of our choice.
So we can be sure to
get an independent opinion.
You understand."
Uncle Al didn't say anything.
"Now," Mrs. Bletcher said,
"I'd like to go up to the house,
if we may, and have a chat
about how Eckhart is doing here."

An hour later
Eckhart sat swinging his legs

over the edge of the deck
while Uncle Al talked
with Mrs. Bletcher in the house.
She had climbed the spiral staircase
to Eckhart's room
and asked him all sorts of prying questions.
How did he spend his days?
Who were his friends?
How did he get along with his uncle?
Eckhart had mumbled brief answers,
which had annoyed Mrs. Bletcher.
He was glad.
He wasn't her business anymore.
Was he?

Eckhart stood up and inched over
to the open window to listen.
"Surely," Mrs. Bletcher was saying,
"surely you've had Eckhart long enough
to decide whether you want to keep him."
"No," Uncle Al said.
Eckhart felt himself shrink
like a wool sock in a dryer.

"The psychologist," Mrs. Bletcher went on,
"that Eckhart saw in Seattle

said he was severely depressed.
To be sure—he'd lost his parents.
But he didn't seem to be recovering,
even four months later.
All those nightmares,
and not getting his strength back
after the pneumonia.
Perhaps . . ." Mrs. Bletcher cleared her throat.
"He has confided in you?"

In the silence that followed,
Eckhart held his breath.
Surely his uncle would not tell
this awful woman
about Hell's Canyon.
Uncle Al said at last, "He's sleeping better
now that he gets fresh air and exercise.
And he has fewer nightmares."
"Hmn," Mrs. Bletcher said.
"I see you have him working in your fields."
"I'm building his strength," Uncle Al replied.
"He's not thin and peaked anymore."

Eckhart was surprised.
Uncle Al sounded like he actually cared,
at least a little.

Mrs. Bletcher said, "I'm sure I agree
that Eckhart looks well.
That's why I think he should be in school
instead of working in your fields."
"We'll see what the doctor says," Uncle Al said.
"Yes," she said, "I'm sure we will."

# Chapter Thirty-Five

On Thursday afternoon
Eckhart and Uncle Al left Sunrise Orchard
for the doctor's appointment
in Wenatchee.
When they passed Pateros,
Eckhart stuck his head out the window
and stared at the Quik Mart.
He imagined Frodo curled up
in the hot case with the cheese fries
as Alicia read to him
from *The Silmarillion*.
Then the Quik Mart was out of sight.
Settling back in his seat,
Eckhart thought,
At least I'm in the front seat this time.
Cub rode in back.

Dr. McCollum examined Eckhart thoroughly

and asked questions
about how much he ate, exercised, and slept.
When she finished,
she twirled her stethoscope and said,
"You're looking well, Eckhart.
Tell me, do you still tire easily?"
"I'm stronger than I was.
But I'm still working on it."
She smiled at him,
and her smile went all the way down
into her eyes,
which were big and brown like Cub's.
There was kindness in them.
"Working how?" she asked.

"I climb a steep hill every day.
My goal is to run up and down the hill
three times in a row without stopping."
Dr. McCollum nodded.
"That sounds like an excellent goal.
Do you still have nightmares?"
"Not as many."
"Want to tell me about them?"
Eckhart shook his head.
There was a silence.

Dr. McCollum spoke softly,

"The accident was a terrible thing."
Eckhart looked down.
He scrunched the white paper
on the examining table tight in his fist.
"Losing your parents," she added,
"and in such an awful way—
It's not something
you'll ever get over, really.
But it is something
you can learn to live with."

Startled, Eckhart looked up at her.
"Exactly. I'm working on that, too—
working hard."
She nodded.
"Don't send me back to school yet," he pleaded.
"I'm too busy working on things—
important things."
Smiling, she slipped her stethoscope back on.
"I can see that. All right, Eckhart.
I think we're done here."

Later that afternoon,
back at Sunrise Orchard,
Eckhart walked over to Uncle Al,
who was standing on a ladder

picking blossoms off one of Lily's peach trees.

Eckhart asked,

"What did Dr. McCollum decide?"

Uncle Al turned. "No school until fall.

Mrs. Bletcher said the 'department'

decided to go along with that."

Uncle Al snorted.

"Yay!" Eckhart jumped in the air.

Uncle Al glanced at him sideways.

"The doctor also said

you should keep on doing

whatever you're doing."


Uncle Al climbed down the ladder,

moved it three feet,

and climbed back up again,

his boots ringing on the metal rungs.

"Why are you picking off blossoms?" Eckhart asked.

Uncle Al pointed. "See how thick they are?

Leave them all on the tree,

and each peach will be as small

as a marble. So I pinch off

three quarters of the blossoms.

Then the remaining ones

can grow big and sweet.

It's called thinning."

"Can I help?" Eckhart asked.

"No."

"But it doesn't look hard."

"It's not." And Uncle Al,

his hands moving fast among the blossoms,

turned his back on Eckhart.

Then Eckhart understood.

These were Lily's trees,

and Uncle Al wanted to tend them by himself.

Feeling lonely and left out,

Eckhart thrust his hands

in his pockets.


For one second

he wondered

if Uncle Al would be friendlier

if he had the violin.

For one second,

as he looked at the peach blossoms,

Eckhart thought he might give up the violin

so the trial would end

and he could stay here for a while.

Then his hands curled into fists

in his pockets.

It's Mom's violin,

he thought fiercely.

Mom's.

Eckhart turned his back on his uncle
and walked away.

# Chapter Thirty-Six

Another week passed,
and the field was at last ready
for the new Honeycrisp trees.
The knip-booms arrived in bins
packed with wet sawdust.
To keep the bare roots damp,
Eckhart watered them three times a day.
Uncle Al started up the tractor
and attached a giant auger.
He drove up to the first red X
sprayed on the dirt
and drilled a big hole in the earth.

At last, it was time to plant.

Eckhart dropped a fertilizer pellet
into the hole,
then scooped some soil on top.

He picked up a little tree
and lowered it gently into the hole.
As he scooped soil over the roots,
he decided he liked planting—
liked working up to his elbows in the soil,
liked the rich smell of it,
liked putting something into the ground
to grow up into the light and air.
Back home in Seattle
they hadn't even had a vegetable garden.
His mom used to plant flowers
in pots and hanging baskets
on the patio.

When the little tree
stood safely in the earth,
Eckhart sat back on his heels
and saw his handprints in the soil
around the trunk.
He looked up at the little tree,
its leaves pattering in the sun.
"You're home," he whispered.
The little tree seemed to wake up
and look around,
as though surprised
to find itself growing in a big empty field—

like the first tree
in the dawn of the world.
Eckhart looked higher,
and saw Heaven's Gate Mountain
waiting to the west.
Soon, he told it.
I'm coming soon.
He smiled,
then moved to the next hole
to plant the next tree.

There were forty-five rows
in the new orchard,
with two hundred red Xs in each row.
Because the Honeycrisp were dwarf trees,
they had to be planted closer together
than the big old Bartlett pear trees.
It was hot work.
They started at six thirty,
in the brief coolness of the morning.
Uncle Al let Eckhart work
four hours a day instead of three,
since it was important to get the trees in fast.
Now that summer was here,
Eckhart did no schoolwork,
so he had lots of time

to spend with Eva, too.

One hot afternoon
she coaxed him down
to a swimming hole in the river,
but Eckhart refused
to go in the water.
With his eyes closed,
with his arms huddled around him,
he sat on the bank
while Eva swam.
He couldn't bear to watch.
The roar of the river
pounded against him,
and he stiffened like a wall
to hold it back.
After a while,
lulled by its endlessness
and by the warmth of the sun,
he began to listen.

Many sounds
made up the river's roar—
a trickling sound,
a lapping sound where the water
caressed the bank,

a spitting sound,
a hissing sound where the water
slithered over small rocks,
a crashing sound where the water
slammed over boulders.
All of these sounds played together
like a river symphony.
This was the first time the river's roar
had reminded him of anything
but death.
Eckhart opened his eyes
to check on Eva.
When he saw her sloshing out of the river,
he sighed with relief.

That night Eckhart dreamed
that his mom was floating
down an endless, gently flowing river
playing her violin
with the river symphony.
Her fingers flew,
and she was smiling
as bright drops of water flew
from her bow.

## Chapter Thirty-Seven

Uncle Al turned off the tractor.
It was the twentieth day of June,
and Eckhart had just planted
the last Honeycrisp tree.
Together they looked over the fledgling orchard.
The rows and rows of little trees
seemed green and glad,
rejoicing that they had found their place
in the world.
Up in the sky
the sun stretched
as though roused from a dream of blue.
That very morning
Eckhart had run up Stagecoach Hill twice
without stopping.

"We did it, Uncle Al!" Eckhart exclaimed.
"We really did it!

We made an orchard!"
Uncle Al smiled,
the first time he had smiled
since the night of the storm.
"It is a fine sight," he agreed.
"But we're not done yet.
We have to build the trellises,
put in stakes to support the trees,
and paint the trunks."
"Paint the trunks?" Eckhart asked.
Uncle Al explained.
"We slather white latex on them.
"To protect the trees from the sun
and herbicides as they grow up."

Eckhart wondered if Uncle Al
would let him stay long enough
to see the trees grow up.
He wanted to see them grow up.
And for the first time,
Eckhart thought about staying
on Sunrise Orchard for a long time.
As he watched the leaves
on the little trees
wave bravely in the wind,
he asked himself,

Is this my real home?
He wasn't sure.
And there was still the trial,
and the violin.

After dinner that evening,
when Eckhart was outside
burying the table scraps,
he saw Uncle Al walking
through the new orchard—
walking slowly,
with a new lightness in his step.
He stood straighter, too.
Now and then he reached out
and touched one of the trees—
not a touch to do anything,
or to fix anything,
but to glory
and to cherish.

It took three weeks
to build the wire trellises
that would support the branches
when the little trees grew bigger.
It took two more weeks
to drive in the stakes

and paint the trunks.

One Saturday in the middle of July,
Eckhart was walking past the shop
on his way to Eva's house,
when he heard a noise
coming from the camping trailer.
He stopped to listen.
It was a clacking, clicking sound—
the typewriter?

Uncertain,
because he had never heard a typewriter before,
Eckhart peered in the window.
He jumped back
when he saw his uncle typing.
As he hurried on toward Eva's house,
Eckhart wondered if his uncle was writing
about the woman
walking through the peach trees
in the summer heat.

When Eckhart reached the little gate
in the wire fence
between Sunrise Orchard
and Eva's place,

Eva came running with Sirius
along the other side of the fence.
"Eva!" he shouted.
She waved.
After ducking through
the little gate,
and closing it behind him,
Eckhart said, "Guess what?
I ran up and down Stagecoach Hill
three times without stopping!"
"Yes!" Eva exclaimed.
"Then you are ready at last
for the Quest of Heaven's Gate."
She wrinkled her forehead, thinking.
"It should take about four hours
to climb to the top,
and two hours to come back down.
What will you tell your uncle?"

Eckhart scratched Sirius behind the ear.
"He's going to Moses Lake tomorrow
to get some parts for the tractor.
He'll be gone all day."
Eva nodded. "Perfect. I'll meet you
in the Chapel Perilous
tomorrow morning at six o'clock

to prepare you for the quest."
She paused, then added,
"They're predicting record heat tomorrow,
so bring a lot—
I mean *a lot*—of water."

That evening
Eckhart carried his mom's violin
out to the shop.
He climbed up to the second floor
and went into the wood shop.
Lily's chair still sat in the corner—
not one speck of dust on the golden wood.
He set the violin case
on a table, opened it,
and pulled off the tab
around the violin's neck.
Taking a deep breath,
Eckhart lifted
the old violin in his hands.

It felt
as light as laughter.
It felt
as rich as a full heart.
It felt—

like home.

Using a soft, clean cloth
from the case,
Eckhart rubbed the violin
in gentle circles,
careful not to harm
the delicate varnish.
The violin needed to be professionally cleaned
and polished by a luthier—
someone who cared for violins.
For a moment
Eckhart thought of asking
his uncle to arrange that.
Then he shook his head.
If he let the violin out of his hands,
he might never get it back.

Gently he laid the violin
back in the case.
How amazing it would be
to play the violin on top
of Heaven's Gate Mountain.
But he knew the intense heat on the hills
would overwhelm
the humidifier inside the case.

The delicate old instrument
might dry out and crack.
He couldn't risk it.

Eckhart closed the case
and then stood, hesitating.
The shop stayed cooler than the house.
With the record heat predicted,
the violin would be safer here.
But he couldn't let Uncle Al find it.
So Eckhart climbed on a stool
and hid the violin
behind some lumber on a high shelf.

He had just come down
the shop stairs
and passed the tractor
parked in the open bay,
when his uncle stepped out
of the camping trailer.
Uncle Al blinked,
as though a little dazed.
Then he grinned—
actually grinned—
at Eckhart.
"Fine evening, isn't it?" he said.

"Think I'll fix that broken step
on the deck."
And he sauntered away.

Eckhart stared after him,
then glanced through the open trailer door.
On the table,
scattered helter-skelter,
lay a dozen typed pages.

## Chapter Thirty-Eight

The next morning
the rising sun
bannered the day
with purple and gold and blazing red.
As Eckhart approached
the Chapel Perilous,
the air was cool,
but heat would soon blister the land.
Only a few ponderosa pines
grew on the hills for shade.
It would be a long hot climb
to Heaven's Gate.

Wearing her shining white shirt,
Eva stood at the entrance
to the Chapel Perilous.
"Enter, oh squire," she said.
Inside, the white candle

burned brightly on the altar.
Behind it,
leaning against the stone wall,
was a round disk.
Eckhart looked closer.
A painted garland
of stars and moons and leaves
circled the rim.
In the center
was a golden star with five points.

"Wow!" Eckhart exclaimed.
"A pentangle! Just like Sir Gawain
had on his shield when he faced
the Green Knight. . . ."
His voice trailed off.
"Is it," he asked, "a shield?
For me?"
"Yes!" Eva said,
her eyes dancing.
"I made it out of an old
cake pan—just hammered down the sides.
It's for you to take on your quest."

Eckhart stared at the shield,
stared and stared,

and wondered if he were dreaming.
When he had played The Green Knight,
he had never found the shield—
the last knightly tool needed
to break the Black Hand's spell.
Now here it was before him—
and in the Chapel Perilous, no less.

Eva pointed at the shield. "Look.
I drilled a hole through the metal
and attached a cord.
You can sling the shield around your neck.
Before you put it on, though,
we must bless it and you.
Let us kneel."

They both knelt
before the altar,
and Eva held up her arms.
"We call on the spirits of the canyon
to guide Eckhart on his noble quest.
We call on Good Wizard.
We call on Lily's pearls.
We call on the magical power
in the pentangle,
whose five points represent

the Greater Powers
of Love, Hope, Truth, Imagination,
and, most of all, Courage.
May these powers walk with Eckhart
on the Quest for Heaven's Gate.
In God we trust.
Amen."
"Amen," Eckhart said.

When they stood up,
Eva slipped the cord on the shield
over Eckhart's head.
Then she lowered the shield
until it rested over his heart.
She stepped back. "Perfect!
Now, do you have enough water?"
"Three bottles," he said,
"and a peanut butter sandwich."
She shook her head.
"You'll need more water.
Take these."
And she stuffed
three more bottles into his pack.
"They're heavy, but you'll need them.
Now, are you ready?"
Eckhart nodded.

Lifting the screen of green boughs,
Eva stepped out of the Chapel Perilous.
Eckhart followed,
blinking in the bright light
after the dimness of the chapel.
Eva held up a tiny blue box.
"This is for you."
When Eckhart opened it,
he saw a white bead nestled
in a scrap of blue velvet.
He smiled. "One of Lily's pearls?"
She nodded. "To protect you on your quest."
"Thanks." Eckhart put the box
deep in his pocket.

Eva looked solemn. "Go forth now,
oh squire, upon your quest.
And may you find what you seek."
"I will well," he said.
Eckhart turned and walked away
through Wizard's Meadow.
Dry weeds bent and scraped
against his jeans.
He looked back and saw Eva
still watching him,
her white shirt shining

against the green boughs
of the Chapel Perilous.
She lifted her hand and waved.
He waved back,
and then turned his face
toward Heaven's Gate.

## Chapter Thirty-Nine

Eckhart passed the ruins
of the Tower of Troth
but didn't look at the creek.
This time, he vowed, I won't fail.
When he reached
the end of Wizard's Meadow,
he stopped to wave at Good Wizard
up on the hill.
He wondered if his 3DS
was still cradled in the gnarled roots.
On he went,
through the second stand of aspens
and into what Eva called Nimue's Meadow.
It ended at the bottom
of Heaven's Gate Mountain.

The trail ended too.

Smaller hills,
the mountain's ribs,
rose higher and higher—
a lumpy stairway to Heaven's Gate.
At the very top,
tiny and far away,
stood a cluster of ponderosa pines.
That was where he had to go.

He started up.

The first hill was easy,
and the second one too.
With his feet scuffing clouds of dust,
Eckhart scrambled around
the sagebrush and bitterbrush.
There was no water up here,
no sign of water at all.
The thought made him thirsty,
so he stopped
for his first water break.

After drinking long and deep,
he looked back.
How little ground he had covered!

Already the heat
seemed like a living thing,
sapping his strength,
and it would only grow hotter—
record heat, Eva had said.
For the first time
doubt crept over him.
Then a meadowlark sang—
a trill long and clear and bright.
It gave him strength.
Eckhart took a last swig,
then stowed his water bottle,
and started climbing again.

Pacing himself,
he scaled the next two hills more slowly.
He was fingering the shield
Eva had made him,
and wishing he had
Sir Gawain's horse, Gringolet,
to carry him up the mountain,
when he heard the rattle.

Eckhart leaped back.

Not five feet away,

coiled on a pile of rocks,
a rattlesnake glared at him
with its head raised.
A forked tongue hissed.
Black diamonds glinted
on its olive-gray back.
Eckhart stepped away again,
and then again,
frightened and fascinated
by the snake.
Still shaking its rattle,
the snake dropped its head
and melted away
into a crevice between the rocks.
Eckhart skirted the rock pile
and resolved to pay more attention
to where he put his feet.

The higher he climbed,
the hotter it grew
as the morning dwindled
toward noon.
The way seemed endless.
Eckhart trudged over a hill
and saw three bucks
with magnificent racks.

He froze.

The wind was blowing toward him,
so they didn't catch his scent.
Once or twice,
as he watched them graze,
their heads swung up sharply
and they stared at him.
When he didn't move,
the bucks nosed the grass again.
Next spring he and Uncle Al
might go shed hunting
and find the bucks' antlers—
If I'm still here, Eckhart thought.

He sneezed.

In a blur of hoof and hide and horn,
the three bucks sprang away,
bounding up the hill.
Eckhart looked after them longingly.
If only he could climb as easily.

On he went—
up and up and up.
After another half hour of climbing,

Eckhart's legs began to ache
and his heart to pound
from the strain of relentlessly plodding uphill.
The sun, swinging higher,
hurled heat from the sky.

He took another water break
in the shade of a scruffy pine tree.
The water was warm now,
but he drank greedily,
finishing his second bottle.
With his eyes, he measured the distance
to the top of Heaven's Gate.
Still a long way to go.

To the north
the ridge of the mountain
sloped down to a kind of notch.
From there
he would be able to see
over to the other side.
Maybe he didn't have to go all the way
to the top after all.

But what would he tell Eva?

He couldn't tell her
he'd failed the Quest of Heaven's Gate.
Maybe he could lie.
Then Eckhart remembered
how a man had tempted Sir Gawain to lie
to avoid facing the Green Knight.
But Sir Gawain refused.
He said that running away
would make him a coward
even if nobody ever knew.
A line from *The Boy's King Arthur*
flashed into Eckhart's mind:
*Ye must encourage yourself,*
*or else ye be all shent*—ruined.

Eckhart held up his shield.
Back in the candlelit Chapel Perilous,
the metal had glinted.
But out here
under the sun,
the shield flashed—
shining
so brightly,
he blinked.

He touched each of the five points

on the pentangle—
love, hope, courage, imagination,
and truth.
Eva had made it.
He stood up
and shouted to the hills,
"I'm not a liar!
I'm not a coward!"
Then, shouldering his backpack,
Eckhart climbed on.

## Chapter Forty

Steadily,
doggedly,
Eckhart tramped up the side of the mountain.
He scuffled through clumps
of dead
sun daisies—
their season long past,
their dry leaves clacking like bones.
He found himself longing
for water,
falling into a dream
of water,
and imagined he was swimming
in a pool, a lake, a river—
no.

A breeze sprang up
but brought little relief

from the heat
almost glistening in the air.
Eckhart emptied the fourth water bottle.
Wiping sweat from his eyes,
he looked up.
Was the top of Heaven's Gate
getting closer?
Again, he went on—
up and up and forever up.

Despite his sunglasses,
his baseball cap,
and his long-sleeved T-shirt,
Eckhart began to feel
as though he were made of sunlight—
carried up the mountain
by sunlight—
forged
by sunlight,
as a knight's sword
is forged
by fire.

He remembered
what his mom had said
after playing Bach's Chaconne on her violin:

*That is the cry*
*of a shining soul*
*as it rises—*
*fighting its way toward heaven.*

As Eckhart climbed,
he knew something
that he hadn't know before.
There had to be strength
in that soul—
strength and fierceness.
There had to be.

The mountain top was close now,
very close.
Above a cliff,
over a rise—
stood the cluster of ponderosas
that he had first spotted
down in the canyon.

Eckhart began to count his steps
as he climbed the last three hundred yards
to Heaven's Gate.
Ten steps, he told himself,
only ten steps—

one,

two,

three. . . .

When he reached ten,

he looked a little way ahead,

and spotted a turtle-shaped rock.

He thought of Frodo,

the turtle,

and of Frodo,

the hero

who had used his last strength

to climb Mount Doom.

I can make it to that rock,

Eckhart told himself.

Just to that rock.

And when he reached the turtle-shaped rock,

he set a new goal.

Ten more steps.

Another rock.


And so it endlessly went.


At last,

when Eckhart thought he couldn't take

one more step,

the shade of the ponderosas

arched over him.
He gasped with relief.
A few more steps
and Eckhart fell to his knees
on the very top
of Heaven's Gate Mountain.

When he found his breath,
he looked out.
Range after range
of blue-gray mountains rose
to the north,
all the way to Canada.
He looked up the valley,
then back the way he had come.
Far below, the orchards
bordering the blue thread of the river
looked like a carpet of green.
Then Eckhart glanced to the south,
and his heart convulsed.

He sprang to his feet.

Not far away
smoke trailed black fingers

along the ground.
A wildfire was burning
across the hills,
and the wind was blowing it
straight down toward Sunrise Orchard.

## Chapter Forty-One

Eckhart stared at the wildfire,
his feet rooted
to the top of Heaven's Gate
as though he were one of the pine trees.
Then he turned
and plunged
back down the way he had come—
running now,
running fast,
sometimes sliding in the loose dirt.
Twice he fell.
He knew he should slow down,
but he didn't.
He knew he should watch for rattlesnakes,
but he didn't.
He knew he should keep drinking water,
but he didn't.
He had to warn his uncle.

Down and down Eckhart flew,
beneath a circling eagle,
and he wished for wings,
shouted
for wings—
for help—
for his uncle—
for Eva.
But there was no one
to hear his shouts—
only the hills,
only the sagebrush,
only the weeds,
only the rocks.

Although Eckhart could no longer see
the fire, he knew it was burning
just over the ridge,
coming,
coming . . .
He skidded to a stop.
If the wind changed
even a little,
he would be in danger.
The fire would race
across the dry face of the mountain

with nothing to stop it
from reaching him.
He should head north,
away from the fire.
But if he did,
Sunrise Orchard would burn.


Then it seemed to Eckhart
that even though he stood
on the flanks of Heaven's Gate,
he was suddenly back
floundering
in the Snake River
at Wild Goose Rapids
in Hell's Canyon.
And in the nightmare
of water
and heat
and fear
and memory,
it seemed
as though he had reached out,
as though he had caught his mom,
and that he was holding her
in his arms,
sobbing—

for her eyes were shut
and her lips were blue
as she whispered,
*You will always be
my knight in shining armor.*

"No!" Eckhart screamed.
The scream brought him back
to where he was
on the side of the mountain.
"By my troth!" he shouted.
And he tore straight down
toward Sunrise Orchard,
his shield bouncing on his chest.

## Chapter Forty-Two

Running as hard as he could,
heaving breaths of ragged air,
it took Eckhart forever
to reach the canyon
and then the gate
in the deer fence.
Now he could see the smoke plume
rising in the sky,
could smell it.
The fire was burning
just over Stagecoach Hill.

Cub howled inside the house.
As Eckhart pounded onto the deck,
shouting—"Uncle Al! Uncle Al!—
he remembered that his uncle
had gone to Moses Lake.

Then why was the front door open?

Eckhart burst into the house.
Uncle Al sprawled
on the sheepskin on the couch,
one arm flung over his face.
On the floor
lay an empty whiskey bottle.
"Uncle Al!" Eckhart shouted.
"There's a wildfire on Stagecoach Hill.
And it's coming straight toward us!"

His uncle blinked
and looked at him with cloudy eyes.
"Today," he said,
his breath reeking of whiskey.
"Four years ago today . . .
Lily died."
His eyes fluttered shut.
"Uncle!" Eckhart shook him.
"Get up. There's a fire!
What should we do?"
Uncle Al frowned. "Fire?"
He sat up,
then fell back on the couch again.
"Lily's peaches . . .

Save the peach trees. . . ."
And he passed out in a dead heap.

Eckhart flew to the door.
The fire now raced
across the top of Stagecoach Hill,
the flames writhing
like red-orange demons.
"What should I do!" Eckhart cried.
There was no phone to call anyone.

He was alone.

The sprinklers,
he thought suddenly.
The sprinklers were his only hope.
The lawn on the south side of the house
stretched some thirty yards
to the bottom of the hill
where Lily's peach trees grew.
Eckhart raced across the lawn
and one by one
turned on the valves
that controlled the water lines
for the lawn sprinklers.
The sprinklers buzzed,

then began to pulse—
sweeping circles of silver water.
Maybe the wet lawn
would create a firebreak.

Then Eckhart looked
at the fledgling Honeycrisp orchard.
It had no firebreak.
Like the peach trees,
the orchard butted against the south hill,
now ablaze with fire.
Eckhart ran to the orchard,
fell to his knees in the dirt,
and opened an irrigation valve.
The sprinklers sprang to life.
He ran through the jetting water
to the next valve
and the next
and the next.
But, to his dismay,
the jets of water
dwindled into trickles.

Suddenly,
as a distant siren wailed,
Eva stood beside him.

"I saw the smoke," she said breathlessly.

"My parents aren't home.

I called 911."

Drenched from the sprinklers,

Eckhart wiped wet hair from his eyes.

"That siren . . . ," he said.

"Is it a fire truck?"

"No," she said.

"That's the siren that calls

the volunteer fire department.

It's not like in the city."

Eckhart stared at the burning hill.

The fire ate its way down,

feeding like a monster

on the dry weeds,

the dead yellow daisies,

the sagebrush,

and the bitterbrush.

"I turned on all the sprinklers," he said,

"but something's wrong.

They're only trickling."

"You have too many on!" Eva exclaimed.

"There isn't enough water pressure

for the orchard and the house and lawn.

You have to choose—
choose between the house and the orchard."

Eckhart's mind raced.
Uncle Al had told him
to save Lily's peach trees.
To do that he had to
leave the lawn sprinklers on
and sacrifice
the new Honeycrisp orchard.
Eckhart looked
over the fledgling orchard,
the leaves on the little trees
fluttering in the same wind
that drove the fire.
As the new orchard had come alive,
so had he,
and so had Uncle Al.
All that work—
the promise and hope
of the future—
How could he let it
turn into a graveyard again?
But if he let Lily's peach trees burn,
Uncle Al would surely send him away,
back to foster care.

Then, as though pierced
by a bright arrow,
Eckhart's heart knew many things at once—
knew
he wanted to stay forever
on Sunrise Orchard—
knew
that Sunrise Orchard
was his real home—
knew
that if he made the right choice now,
he would lose that home
forever.

Eckhart started running.

## Chapter Forty-Three

Wait!" Eva grabbed Eckhart's arm.
"What are you going to do?"
Eckhart stopped.
"Save the new orchard," he said.
"Stay here where it's safe."
And he ran back to the lawn.
Tongues of fire
licked down the hill,
crackling,
hissing,
spitting smoke—
yellow near the ground,
gray-white in the air.

Eckhart began to cough
as he scrambled around
turning off the lawn sprinklers.
Eva did not stay behind

but helped shut them off.
As the water pressure changed,
the sprinklers in the Honeycrisp orchard
whirred to life,
spraying circles of water
pumped from the river.
Water drops caught the sunlight,
glinting silver,
and to Eckhart it was the glint of hope.

The river was going to save them.

Then he looked at the peach trees—
now dry and defenseless
against the fire.
He turned to Eva.
"When will the fire truck get here?"
She coughed. "I don't know.
Probably not in time to save the house."
Eckhart stiffened.
"Uncle Al's passed out in there."
"We have to get him out!" Eva exclaimed.
"One spark blown across the lawn,
and the house will go up—
especially with this wind."

Something roared.
Up on the hill
the fire had ignited
one of the few ponderosa pines.
The tree blazed
like a gigantic torch.
Red and gold flames
leaped upward
from branch
to branch
to branch
as though the wildfire wanted
to singe the very sky.
"Save us!" Eckhart cried.
And he coughed,
and then they were both coughing
from the smoke
crawling down their throats.

They ran into the house.
Eva slapped Uncle Al,
then threw a glass of water on him.
"Wh-what?" he sputtered, coming around.
"There's a fire!" Eckhart shouted.
"We have to get out of the house!"
Uncle Al blinked. "What fire?"

With Eva on one side of Uncle Al
and Eckhart on the other,
they got him off the couch.
Cub ran in circles beside them.
Uncle Al dragged his feet
as they half carried him
out of the house.
When they stepped onto the deck,
the smell of smoke
finally roused him.

They were just in time.
Flames skipped up
the south side of the house.
But Uncle Al was staring
at the blazing pine tree.
"God Almighty!" he cried.
Then the fire jumped
from the hillside,
and flames flickered in the peach trees.
"Lily!" Uncle Al cried.
"Why aren't the lawn sprinklers on?"
He wrenched away,
leaped off the deck,
and ran toward the peach trees.

"No!" Eckhart shouted
as the fire roared.
"Uncle Al! You'll be killed!"
Without thinking,
Eckhart hurled himself off the deck
and ran
straight after his uncle,
straight toward the fire.

## Chapter Forty-Four

A few yards from Lily's burning trees,
Eckhart barreled into Uncle Al
and knocked him to the ground.
Smoke poured over them,
filling Eckhart's eyes,
his nose,
his lungs.
A spark landed on Uncle Al's T-shirt
and flared orange.
Shouting,
Eckhart slapped out the spark
with his hands.
But another spark came—
and another
and another—
Eckhart ripped off his shield
and began beating the sparks.

His T-shirt and jeans were still wet,

but soon he would catch fire too.
Faster and faster
Eckhart swung his shield,
beating out showers of sparks.
The golden pentangle glowed
in the light
from the flames
that roared
like a devouring dragon.

"No!" Eckhart screamed,
hitting the sparks,
coughing,
choking.
"No!"

Voices shouted,
hands pulled at him,
tried to pull him away
from his uncle.
Eckhart fought,
but the smoke grew
too thick
in his lungs—
the heat
too hot

on his face.
"Mom!" he cried.
The fire roared—
or was it the Snake River roaring?

And then Eckhart seemed to dream.
He was clutching a log,
and the Black Hand was dragging him down,
and the river fumed into a river of light,
and a voice sang—
My *knight* . . .
My *knight* . . .
and he let go—

Then, as a violin played
a melody fierce
and chorded with light,
everything began to shine.
Bright,
brilliant,
a sun,
a soul—
shining
he rose,
shining
he knew no more.

# Chapter Forty-Five

Eckhart woke.
Slowly he opened his eyes
and blinked at a strange white ceiling
floating over his head.
He frowned.
Wasn't the ceiling in his bedroom
made of golden wood?
Turning his head,
he saw a window,
a chair,
and in the chair sat Mr. DeHart.
His gold-rimmed glasses
sparkled in the sun
streaming through the window.

Mr. DeHart smiled.
"Awake at last, I see," he said.
"Where am I?" Eckhart asked,

and was startled
by the sound of his hoarse voice,
by the soreness in his throat.
"You're in the hospital in Brewster.
Would you like to sit up?"
Eckhart nodded.
Mr. DeHart pushed a button
that raised the head of the bed.

When Eckhart settled back onto the pillows,
he saw a clamp on his finger
connected by a wire to a machine.
He touched his cheek—
a tube wrapped around his face
and poked into his nose.
"What is this?" he began,
but then he coughed.
"It's an oxygen tube," Mr. DeHart explained.
"You inhaled a lot of smoke."

Then it all came back to Eckhart—
the fire,
his uncle,
the orchard.
"What happened?" he asked,
"My uncle—is he all right?"

Mr. DeHart nodded. "Al is fine.
The doctors are treating him
for smoke inhalation
and a bad burn on his right arm."
"And Eva?" Eckhart asked.
"Not to worry," Mr. DeHart said.
"She heard the fire truck pull up
and ran to tell them
you and your uncle needed help.
She's fine too."
"I feel woozy," Eckhart said.
Mr. DeHart nodded.
"That's from the medicine
the doctor gave you."

Eckhart leaned forward.
"What happened to the house—
and the orchard?"
Mr. DeHart sighed. "The firemen
couldn't save the house.
What's left will have to be torn down.
Fortunately, your uncle was insured.
He can rebuild."
Mr. DeHart peered over his glasses.
"You saved the new orchard, Eckhart.
An interesting choice."

Eckhart was afraid
to ask the next question,
but he had to know.
"What about Lily's peach trees?"
Mr. DeHart shook his head. "Burned."
Eckhart sank back on the pillow
and closed his eyes.
So that was it, then.
His uncle would surely send him away.
He would be in foster care forever—
would have to leave
Sunrise Orchard,
leave
the canyon,
leave
the Chapel Perilous,
leave
Eva—
and everything
that had become his home.

Tears leaked from his eyes.
"There, now," Mr. DeHart said kindly.
"Everything will be all right, son.
Sleep now. The doctors want to keep you

overnight for observation."

The next morning
a nurse rolled Eckhart
out of the hospital in a wheelchair.
Eckhart felt silly,
for he could easily have walked,
but the nurse said it was hospital policy.
Mr. DeHart opened
the back door of his truck.
Uncle Al was already sitting
in the front passenger seat,
a big bandage on his right arm.
He didn't look at Eckhart.

All during the drive home
Mr. DeHart chatted
about the weather,
the apple crop,
and his family's next camping vacation
to Lake Wenatchee.
He explained that Eva
would have come to the hospital too,
but she was busy
planning something for Eckhart.

"Something special," Mr. DeHart added.

Neither Eckhart nor Uncle Al said a word.

Eckhart wondered
what had happened to his shield.
The hospital had probably thrown it away.
He wished
he were wearing it now,
for he felt
adrift,
lost,
and alone,
and needed protection.
He didn't know
what was going to happen to him now.

## Chapter Forty-Six

When Mr. DeHart turned up the road
to Sunrise Orchard,
Uncle Al got out
and opened the gate.
They drove up the hill,
and Eckhart's heart lifted a little
at the sight of the Honeycrisp orchard.
The little trees stood
straight and tall,
their green leaves fluttering
as though in greeting and thanks.
Uncle Al looked at them too.

They pulled up to the shop,
untouched by the fire,
and got out of the truck.
Eckhart looked toward the house,
but the blue spruce trees

hid it from sight.
"Well," Uncle Al said,
"might as well know the worst."
And he started down the path.
Eckhart and Mr. DeHart followed.
As they walked around the blue spruce trees,
Eckhart's breath came fast
as he steeled himself
for the sight ahead.
Still, when he saw the house—
or what was left of it—
he gasped.

The black walls gaped
with raggedy holes,
as though some monster hand
had torn out great chunks.
The stink of smoke
soured the air.
Soot-blackened, the antler trees
still clacked in the breeze.
The metal roof tipped
over the collapsed walls
of Eckhart's bedroom.
All of his stuff would be ruined.
"Mom's violin!" he exclaimed,

starting toward the door.
Mr. DeHart grabbed him.
"It's too dangerous!"
Then Eckhart remembered.
"I took it to the wood shop," he said, relieved.
"The violin's in the wood shop."

Slowly,
dreading what he would see,
Eckhart looked past the house
at the scorched hillside.
Lily's peach trees stood
like four black skeletons,
the leaves all burned away.

Eckhart felt his heart sink
down and down,
so far down
that if he threw up—
for his stomach was heaving—
he feared his heart
might spill out too.

Mr. DeHart was speaking to Uncle Al.
"Won't you reconsider?
You and Eckhart are welcome

to stay with us on Acadia Orchard
for as long as you need."
Uncle Al shook his head. "Thank you.
I do appreciate that, but no.
We'll camp out in the trailer
until we decide what to do next."
Eckhart stared at the ground,
one hand on his stomach.
Mr. DeHart nodded. "Well,
if you need anything,
anything at all,
you know where to find me."

He turned to Eckhart.
"Eva said she'd meet you
in the usual place in the canyon
at eleven o'clock."
Mr. DeHart glanced at his watch.
"It's almost eleven now," he added.
"Can I go?" Eckhart asked,
without looking at Uncle Al.
"All right," Uncle Al said.

Eckhart walked around
the burned-out house,
across the singed lawn,

and opened the gate in the deer fence.
As he walked up Stagecoach Road,
he thought,
This may be the last time
I ever go up the canyon.

The fire had spared the canyon.

He walked slowly,
partly because his lungs were still
raw from the smoke,
and partly because he wanted
to take in everything—
the ponderosas swaying,
the aspen leaves like green coins
click-clacking in the wind,
the grouse thumping,
the quail skittering.
He loved the canyon,
loved Sunrise Orchard,
and couldn't bear to lose either one.

Through the trees
he glimpsed
Heaven's Gate Mountain
to the west,

and stopped.
I climbed to the top,
he thought in amazement.
To the very top.

Then into his mind
came the memory
of how he had run toward the fire
to save his uncle.
"I didn't even think," Eckhart said.
"I just did it."
He thought of his dad
diving from the safety of the boulder
into the Snake River.
"He didn't know," Eckhart whispered,
staring up at Heaven's Gate.
"Dad didn't know I'd be left all alone.
He just tried to save Mom.
That's all."

And Eckhart walked on up the canyon.

## Chapter Forty-Seven

When he reached
the Chapel Perilous,
Eva was waiting outside
in her shining white shirt.
"Eckhart!" she cried. "How are your lungs?"
He shrugged.
Then he blurted, "I'm afraid
Uncle Al will send me back
to foster care.
He barely said a word to me."
Eva's eyes blazed.
"But you saved his life!"

Eckhart stared at her.
"I did?" he asked slowly.
She nodded. "The firemen said you did."
Something in Eckhart's heart
grew suddenly warm,

and he smiled.
He felt as though he were sparkling
from head to toe.
"I did save his life," he said, amazed.
"I really did!"
Then his smile faded,
the sparkle faded.
"But Uncle Al doesn't think much of me,
I guess."

"So what!" Eva exclaimed.
"It doesn't matter what he thinks of you.
It matters what you think of yourself."
Eckhart stared at her.
Stern,
fierce,
she almost shimmered in her white shirt.
She asked, "Did you make it to the top
of Heaven's Gate?
Did you fulfill your quest?"

Eckhart stood tall,
and when he answered her,
his voice rang out true and strong—
"I did."
Eva nodded solemnly. "Then it's time

for the ceremony."
"What ceremony?"
Her eyes danced.
"You'll see. Come inside.
Everything's ready."
She lifted the screen,
and they stepped inside
the Chapel Perilous.

The white candle
burned brightly on the altar,
now strewn with white roses.
Eckhart's eyes grew wide
when he saw what lay beside them.
"My shield!" he exclaimed.
Eva smiled. "My dad saved it for you."
Eckhart picked up the shield.
Here and there
the sparks had burned
the paint off the metal,
so spots of black-edged silver
shone on the golden star.

Eva said, "I almost painted over
those burn marks. But then I thought
they were like badges of your ordeal."

Eckhart nodded. "I like seeing
the silver metal shining through."
Eva took the shield.
"The cord was burned,
so I put this red ribbon on instead."
She slipped the ribbon over his neck
and placed the shield over his heart.
"Now kneel," Eva said.
He did.

Eva picked up a long flat stick,
wrapped with duct tape at one end
to make a silver handle.
On the handle
a red stone banded with gold
shone like a ruby.

Eva held the stick high.
"For your valor," she began,
"and for your courage
in the face of certain death—
I, Evangeline,
Lady of the Canyon,
name thee
Eckhart the Lion Heart.

And in the name
of God,
Saint Michael,
Saint George,
and especially Good Wizard,
I make thee a knight."
And Eva tapped the stick
against Eckhart's right shoulder
and then his left shoulder
and then his right shoulder again.

"Rise, Sir Eckhart!" she cried.

But Eckhart stayed on his knees
looking up at her,
his heart bright
with joy.
When at last he rose to his feet,
he said, "Thanks."
How he wished
he could stay here with her forever.
Eva seemed to read his mind.
"We can't let your uncle send you away."
"I'm not going to lose another best friend."

Eckhart asked, his voice husky,

"I'm your best friend?"
Eva smiled. "Seems Good Wizard
did give me my heart's desire."
"Even though," Eckhart said,
"I might have to . . . go away?"
She nodded. "I'd rather have you
for a best friend for one day,
than someone else forever."
And suddenly,
as they looked at each other,
their eyes held
in a strange new way.
Eckhart's heart jumped oddly.
Eva's cheeks turned bright pink.
"We won't let your uncle send you away,"
she said fiercely. "We won't!"

# Chapter Forty-Eight

Late that afternoon
Eckhart lifted his mom's violin
out from behind the stack of lumber
in the shop.
He set the case on the workbench
and opened it.
The violin looked fine,
except for an old scratch
near the sounding board.
Eckhart smiled.
Once he had asked his mom
why she didn't have that fixed.
"Because," she'd said,
"the violin came to me with that scratch.
Imperfections add character,
like a scar or wrinkle on someone's face."

Maybe, Eckhart thought,

looking down at the scratch,
we all have imperfections.
He was glad he had at last told Eva
about his—
about Hell's Canyon.
Eva, being Eva,
had listened intently,
gravely—
her eyes emerald stars,
her face framed
by the winged unicorn
on the chapel wall.
And she had understood.

Eckhart picked up the old violin—
how fragile it was,
and yet how strong.
He placed the violin on his shoulder.
When his chin touched the chin rest—
where his mom's chin had so joyfully rested—
he said, "It's all right, Mom.
It's all right."

Taking a breath,
Eckhart raised the bow
and played a long A.

The violin was sadly out of tune.

So he took the pitch pipe

out of the case,

blew into it,

and turned the pegs

that tightened the strings.

The song his mom had written for him—

set to Bach's Chaconne—

sang in his head.

With it came a rush of sadness.

But that sadness, Eckhart knew,

was only one part of him now,

not all of him.


When the violin was back in tune,

he played the first line:


    *Come along home . . .*


Eckhart stopped—

lifting the bow abruptly.

His arms sagged.

After all he had done,

after all he had been through,

he still didn't have a home.

He needed to talk to Uncle Al.

Eckhart carried the violin outside.
Uncle Al stood beside the camping trailer,
barbecuing hot dogs on the grill.
Beside it a big wooden wire spool
made a round table
covered with paper plates,
bottles of mustard and ketchup,
a jar of pickles,
and buns spilling from a package.
But there was only one chair,
a folding chair.

Only one chair.

Eckhart stopped.
He stared at that chair
and stared at it,
his heart pounding so hard,
he thought it might explode,
thought he might explode.
His hand shaking,
he pointed the bow
straight at Uncle Al.

"I saved your life!" Eckhart exclaimed.

"Saved—

your—

life!"

Uncle Al looked up,

then down,

and turned the hot dogs on the grill.

Fat sputtered in the flames,

and Cub sat up, sniffing.

"I'm sorry," Uncle Al said at last.

"Sorry?" Eckhart asked, confused.

Uncle Al nodded. "Sorry I got drunk

and almost got us both killed."

He looked straight into Eckhart's eyes.

"I'm proud of what you did, Eckhart.

Your parents would be proud too."


Eckhart blinked.

It was the first time

Uncle Al had ever called him by his name.

Then Uncle Al added,

"I've got something for you,

something that should belong to you now."

He went into the trailer

and came out carrying a chair.

Lily's chair.

The golden oak,
newly oiled,
gleamed in the sunshine.
The curling sunburst carved on the back
glimmered a darker gold.
Eckhart just stared at it.
"For me?" he asked slowly.
Uncle Al nodded. "For you, Eckhart."

"Then . . ." Eckhart swallowed hard.
"Then you're not . . .
not going to send me back to foster care?"
Uncle Al grinned. "If I did that,
who'd look after this place?
The trial is over.
You can stay on Sunrise Orchard—
if, that is, you want to."
He turned the hot dogs again.
"I got a letter from your aunt Barbara.
She's earned her doctorate
in computer science
and has a fine new job in Seattle.
She said she'd take you in,
if you'd rather."

Uncle Al watched him.

Eckhart blinked.
A doctorate in computer science?
That meant Aunt Barbara
would have everything—
blazing-fast Internet,
the newest computers,
the latest software.
He could game again,
could have something of his old life back. . . .

Then a meadowlark called.

Eckhart looked out
at the fledgling Honeycrisp orchard—
looked out
at the canyon where he'd found a best friend—
looked out
at Heaven's Gate Mountain
rising to the west.
And he knew
he wouldn't trade anything
for all of this.

But there was one more thing—

his mom's violin.

Eckhart lifted his chin.
"Uncle Al," he said. "It's my fault
the house burned down—
because I saved the orchard instead.
Here." Taking a deep breath,
Eckhart held out the violin.
"You can sell this
to pay for rebuilding the house."

Uncle Al looked at him for a long moment,
the sun showing every wrinkle on his face.
"I appreciate that, Eckhart.
But the fire wasn't your fault.
I'm glad you chose the orchard.
And I wouldn't take that violin from you
if I were starving. Keep it,
and remember your mom.
We'll get you started on some lessons this fall."
He slapped two hot dog buns
on the grill and added,
"Now, why don't you sit down
and play us something
before dinner?"

Eckhart smiled.
He pulled Lily's chair—
his chair now—
up to the round table.
When he sat down,
his feet now touched the ground.
He planted them firmly,
tucked the violin under his chin,
and began to play.

> *Come along home*
> *my shining son,*
> *over the hill*
> *with the rising sun . . .*

# Also by Dia Calhoun

*Eva of the Farm*

*Firegold*

*Aria of the Sea*

*White Midnight*

*The Phoenix Dance*

*Avielle of Rhia*

*The Return of Light: A Christmas Tale*